This book should be returned to any branch of the
Lancashire County Library on or before the date shown

To Mum and Dad

Guy Bass

To my weird and wonderful studio-family
at Dynamo, for the best support
and inspiration EVER

Oda

STRIPES PUBLISHING
An imprint of Little Tiger Press
1 The Coda Centre, 189 Munster Road,
London SW6 6AW

A paperback original
First published in Great Britain in 2014

Text copyright © Guy Bass, 2014
Illustrations copyright © Dynamo, 2014

ISBN: 978-1-84715-464-4

A CIP catalogue record for this book is
available from the British Library.

Printed and bound in the UK.

2 4 6 8 10 9 7 5 3 1

FROG
the
BARBARIAN

Guy Bass

stripes

Who's Who in Kingdomland

FROG
Alien Prince, self-proclaimed saviour of the world, rebel without a pause, wielder of the invincible magic sword Basil Rathbone.

BUTTERCUP
Frog's best friend who raised him from an egg and kept him safe at The Edge of the End of the World, keeper of secrets.

SHERIFF EXPLOSION
Frog's trusty yet reluctant steed.

THE RAREWOLF
Ancient beast, guardian of the world and god of the storms, last of his kind, bit of a grump.

THE MYSTERY KROAKAN
?

PRINCESS RAINBOW
Heir to the throne of
Kingdomland, daughter of the
King and Queen of Everything,
wearer of sparkly dresses.

**THE QUEEN OF
KINGDOMLAND**
Champion-choosing
Empress of Everything.

**THE KING OF
EVERYTHING**
Muddle-minded King
of Kingdomland.

MAN-LOR
Furry-panted, barbarian
protector of Princess Rainbow,
secret writer of poetry.

CAPTAIN CAMPERLASH
Red-faced and rage-filled
Captain of the Royal
Guard.

GENERAL KURG
Captured commander
of the 513th Kroakan
invasion fleet, failed
space invader.

NIGEL THE BRAGON
Bafflingly boastful Enemy
of Kingdomland.

Gone But Not Forgotten:

THE WIZARD OLDASDUST
Kingdomland's royal wizard, adviser to
Princess Rainbow, caster of spells, wearer of
impractically tall hats.

Once Upon
the End of the World...

The ~~Incredibul~~ ~~Amazing~~ Astownding Legend of Prince Frog

The Next Chapter of the Rest of the Advenchur Continues

One upon a tyme there was a prince called FROG. Ackshully he was called ROYUL MAJESTY, LORD OF ALL KINGDUMS, RITEFUL ROOLER OF THE WURLD, PRINCE FROG! but that takes ages to rite down.

So, Prince Frog came out of a goldun egg in a royal lake. He was mighty and green and had jumping legs for jumping and the most skills by a milliun.

And Frog was supposed to rool over all of Kingdomland just like the KING AND

QUEEN OF EVERYTHING. It was his ~~density~~ destiny. But the Wurld had Ended so Frog had to live on a farty little Island with his best frend BUTTERCUP. And then Frog desided to go and see what the End of the Wurld looked like and he fownd out the wurld was not ackshully ended and there was stuff and things everywhere! He was really pleased because it ment that his hole life was going to be shined-up crowns and polished sandwitches. And then Frog went to the royal palase but there was alreddy a prinsess on the throne. She was called Prinsess Rainbow but Frog called her Prinsess BrainSlow. Hahahahahaha!

And then she locked ~~me~~ Frog in a cage. And then Prinsess BrainSlow (hahaha) said Frog you're Not Eaven Ackshully a Reel Prince at All! Frog had had enough of

Prinsess BrainSlow (haha) so he escaped from his cage using his magic ninja skills. Then he fownd the royal lake where he came from and he went for a swim. And then he accidentelly woke up some owter space alien invaiders. They were called KROAKANS and they looked qwite a lot like Frog. Their Leeder was called JENERAL KURG and he told Frog that he was supposed to rule the hole wurld because Frog was akshully an owter-space alien prince and was the son of KING KROAK. So Frog was really pleased again. In your face Prinsess!

And then Frog found owt he was supposed to skortch the earth and blackun the skyes and DISTROY THE WHOLE WURLD. The Kroakans prooved it by Ka-sploding up the royal palase to bits.

Frog said STOP I DON'T WANT TO DISTROY THE WHOLE WORLD, PRINCES ARE MENT TO BE GOOD so he defeeted Jeneral Kurg and the Kroakans by being mighty and saved the prinsess and probubly the whole wurld. It was a big day.

After that Frog said goodbye to the prinsess and the little bit of palase that was left. He desided he didn't ever want to rool anything any more. He didn't ever want to sit on a throne in the palase and he didn't ever want to distroy the wurld like an alien space invaider.

He was not going to do any of those things, ever again.

So what was he going to do?

The Big Question

Frog closed his book and chewed on the piece of chalk in his hand.

"That's the big question, isn't it?" he said. "What *am* I going to do now?"

He sat up and looked around. It was a cool, breezy afternoon and the sun and three moons hung in the sky. To the east was a dense forest of blue-leaved trees; to the west, crimson-red hills gave way to a range of jagged mountains, jutting into a fog of cloud. Frog watched a family of giant oak-folk make their way across the distant horizon, as ancient as the trees they carried on their backs. Nearby, yapping bark larks dived for whistle fish in a trickling river. Frog glanced over at the sheep grazing lazily on the riverbank.

"What would you do, Sheriff Explosion?" Frog asked, hopping over to his trusty steed. He tore a clump of lime-green grass from the bank and fed it to the sheep. "I mean, if you didn't want to be a prince but you were still definitely the mightiest, most skilled-up outer space someone in Kingdomland and probably the whole, entire universe? Would you just let all that mightiness go to waste?"

"Baa," replied Sheriff Explosion.

"Neither would I," replied Frog. He peered into the river; his reflection stared expectantly back. His round, hairless head and bulbous, yellow eyes suddenly seemed strange and otherworldly … his bright green skin decidedly extraterrestrial.

"Buttercup will know what I'm supposed to do — she always makes the right choice," he concluded. "I've met princesses, wizards, barbarians, aliens ... but Buttercup's still my only real friend."

"Baa?" Sheriff Explosion bleated.

"You're a trusty steed – that's different," replied Frog.

"Baa," the sheep sighed.

"Anyway, I still need to tell Buttercup the world hasn't ended," Frog added. "So, we follow the river until we reach the giant waterfall in the sky – then it's a quick froggy-paddle to the— Wuh?"

Frog had spotted something in the river – a small, oil-black orb. At first he thought it was submerged under the water but as he peered closer he realized it was a reflection. He spun around and looked up. The orb hovered in mid-air above him, rotating constantly on its axis, emitting a low, breathy hum and sparking with green light.

"Baa?" said Sheriff Explosion.

"What *is* that?" murmured Frog, as the spinning orb buzzed around him like a bumbleflea. It swooped under his legs and over his head – then stopped dead in the air, inches from his face. Frog reached out a hand to touch it.

WHiiiiiiSHT–SHUNG!

Frog felt something whistle past his head and the orb vanished before his eyes. He turned to see it pinned against a tree, a long arrow protruding from the trunk.

"Yoiks…" squeaked Frog. He edged towards the tree as the orb fizzed its last. Cautiously, he reached out and stroked the arrow's feathered tip. "That's skilled-up aiming … unless that arrow was aimed at me. Hey! *Was* that arrow aimed at me?"

Frog looked behind him — and then up
and up, over the top of the blue forest,
following the arrow's trajectory. There,
standing motionless on the edge of a high,
crescent-shaped rock, was a great, grey wolf,
as big as a horse.

"The rarewolf!" Frog cried. He had met the rarewolf when he first arrived in Kingdomland, when the beast had droned on about some ancient prophecy of doom. Indeed he was so unpleasant that Frog thought he might have to defeat him then and there. But then the rarewolf helped Frog vanquish the Kroakan invaders. Frog wasn't sure what to think. He peered closer.

Squinting, he could make out a green-skinned figure in a long, hooded robe, perched upon the rarewolf's back. He had seen the figure once before, sitting atop the rarewolf moments after Frog saved Princess Rainbow and probably the whole world. But this time he could see exactly what it was.

A Kroakan.

An outer space alien invader.

"Who the ... who?"

This wasn't like any Kroakan he'd seen before — she was smaller and leaner, with two long antennae protruding from her forehead. She adjusted a longbow on her shoulder and gave Frog a nod. Then the rarewolf huffed and began to slope away.

"Wait! Come back!" Frog cried. He turned to his sheep. "My big bucket of questions is bursting, Sheriff! Who is the mystery Kroakan? Why is she riding the rarewolf? What if she's put some *evil psychic space eye* on him and turned him into her trusty slave? Badness! Grab your things, Sheriff Explosion!"

Frog quickly collected all his worldly goods. They numbered:

One journal, in which Prince Frog recorded his adventures in the third person.

One sunder-gun, Prince Frog's outer space alien invader ray gun.

One invincible magic sword (formerly a stick) named Basil Rathbone.

He holstered his sword and sunder-gun and shoved his journal into the back of his catastrophe pants – his supposedly End of the World-proof shorts.

"Let's go — the chase is on!" cried Frog, and disappeared into the forest.

"Baa…" sighed Sheriff Explosion.

The Picnic

"This way!" cried Frog, racing through the forest. He had to find out the truth about the mystery Kroakan. He leaped and swung his way through the dense maze of branches. "We're getting closer! I can almost smell the rarewolf's stinky—"

Frog thrust himself between two branches … and emerged in mid-air.

"EEEEEEEEEEEEEEEEEEEEEEEEEE EEEE—"

Sposh.

Water engulfed him, filling his nose and mouth. Frog curled into a ball, remembering how to breathe underwater. He looked around and found himself in the centre of a small, shallow lake. It struck him that the last

24

time he'd gone swimming, he had discovered a spaceship and inadvertently awakened a murderous alien army that tried to bring about The End of the World.

He decided it was probably best to swim for shore.

Frog dodged a flurry of grasping hookweeds and swam towards the bank. He burst out of the water and stumbled on to dry land.

"Calamity! The sky falls!" cried a voice. "It's the End of the World!"

Frog blew water out of his nostrils and earholes and looked back. He was in a clearing at the base of a small waterfall. A stout ball of a man with a once-splendid red coat, an unkempt grey beard and skin like an old potato was jumping up and down as if his feet were on fire. Below him, sitting upon a large blanket next to a lavish picnic, was a tall woman with cascading copper hair and brightly embroidered finery. She peered at Frog with a look of perplexed impatience.

"The final day! The End is nigh!" the old man wailed.

"Do hush, poppet," said the woman, rising gracefully to her feet and smoothing down her dress. "The world is not ending — nor was it last time, or the time before that. And the only thing falling from the sky is that pond-gobbin over there."

The woman pointed at Frog, as he got to his feet.

"A gobbin, you say?" murmured the round old man, halting his fearful jig in mid-air. "O joy! O glorious stay of execution!"

"Sorry to disappoint," Frog began, hoisting up his catastrophe pants, "but I'm not a gobbin. I am..."

Frog realized he had never spoken his name without the inclusion of his various princely titles. He put his fists on his hips and took a deep breath:

"I am Frog!"

"If I say you are a gobbin, you are a gobbin," the tall woman declared. "Now be gone, before my husband wreaks terrible, savage revenge upon you for interrupting our picnic."

"Who, him?" scoffed Frog.

"Who, me?" blurted the old man.

"Pfff — no offence, but you need to take a closer look at all the mightiness I've got going on," added Frog. "I could defeat that old butterball with my toes. I'd move into a house of victory and use him as the welcome mat!"

"Oh dear," sighed the old man, as Frog felt the woman's glare.

"Husband, be a poppet and fetch my longsword," she said, cracking her knuckles. "I'm going to chop off this gobbin's head."

The Shyclops

"Oh dear, oh dear," the old man muttered, shuffling from foot to foot. "Chop chop…"

"My sword, husband," insisted the woman. "It's in the picnic basket. Next to the porkberry pie."

"Wait, you're really picking a fight with me?" asked Frog. "OK, then I promise not to use all of my mightiness on you – it wouldn't be fair." He reached down to his scabbard and wrapped his fingers around the handle of his sword. "Behold … Basil Rathbone!" Frog drew out the gleaming, magical blade with a flourish. "He's the only sword with his own song!" he cried. "But you're not allowed to sing along."

With that, Frog took a deep breath…

The Basil Rathbone Song

Basil Rathbone!
Most Powerful Sord in Kingdumland
Basil Rathbone!
Everyone say Oooh and gather rownd!
He can slice through iron or a blayde of grass
You're bownd to be imppressed by his sharp-i-ness
Basil Rathbone!
Most Powerful Sord in Kingdumland
Basil Rathbone!

He sometimes makes a swishing sownd
Changed from a stick in seconds flat
By a dying wizard with a verry tall hat
Basil Rathbone!
Most Powerful Sord in Kingdumland
Basil Rathbone! The sord that I own!
Basil Rathbone! He's never on loan!
Yeah yeah yeah yeah (fade out)

The woman's eyes grew wide. The round old man shrieked in horror. Frog grinned.

"Pretty intimidating, isn't it?" he chuckled. "Basil Rathbone's the most first-rate, magically unbreakable sword ever. I bet you've never ... seen ... anything—"

A dark shadow fell over Frog, and he realized that the looks of horror on the man and woman's faces may not have been in response to Basil Rathbone. Slowly, he turned back towards the lake.

A monster had emerged from behind the waterfall, and now loomed over him. This fat, burly brute was as tall as a house, with tufts of hair dotted all over its body, four great arms (each carrying a tree-trunk club) and a single eye in the middle of its forehead.

"DON'T LOOK AT ME!" it bellowed.

Frog saw a club rush towards him and

then found himself flying through the air. The impact was so hard he felt the breath leave his body. He slammed into a tree and crumpled to the ground, head spinning and ears ringing.

"The Beast of the Apocalypse! The End is upon us!" shrieked the old man as the creature lumbered out of the water towards him.

"No, it's a *shyclops!*" cried the woman. "They cannot stand to be watched – do not look it in the eye!"

"STOP JUDGING ME! DON'T LOOK AT ME!" the beast cried.

Frog opened his eyes. He sat up and checked that he was still in one green piece.

"Ow…" he said, rubbing his head. He looked up to see the old man frozen in terror as the shyclops loomed over him.

The man just had time to mutter "It's the End of the—" before the shyclops kicked him to the ground with its giant foot.

"Husband!" cried the woman and raced, screaming, towards the shyclops. The stunned beast stumbled backwards, swinging its clubs wildly. The woman was swift and agile, dodging the first two swings, but the third struck her a glancing blow across the head. As she fell limply to the ground, the beast raised all four clubs above its head...

Frog looked down to see his magical sword still gripped tightly in his hand.

"Hey! Pick on someone your own mightiness!" he cried, bounding towards the shyclops in great hops.

"TOO CLOSE...!" the shyclops boomed.

Frog activated his kroak cloak. His mysterious camouflage ability rendered him all but invisible. Only his catastrophe pants could be seen. It was more than enough to embarrass the shyclops even further.

"AWAY! GET AWAY!" The mortified beast flailed its clubs wildly.

The invisible Frog sprang upwards, grabbing a club as it sped past his head. It propelled him skywards. He spiralled in the air before landing squarely on the back of the shyclops's neck.

"NO! LEAVE ... ME ... ALONE!"

"Stop doing an evil monster rampage and I will!" insisted Frog, reappearing as he clung on desperately to one of the creature's hair tufts. The shyclops stomped and flailed in panic but couldn't shake off its determined green passenger.

"This is just a taste of my mightiness pie!" insisted Frog. "Don't make me feed you the whole thing!"

"ALONE! ALONE!" the beast roared — and swung all of its clubs towards its own head.

THUD.

With that, the shyclops fell to the ground, unconscious.

"Whole pie ... it is," panted Frog, hopping down from the shyclops' back.

"W-we're alive?" blurted the old man, getting to his feet. "It's not the End?"

"It appears not," said the woman, inspecting the bump on her head as she strode towards Frog. "That was impressive work, pond-gobbin — a shyclops who feels judged is a fearsome opponent... We have lost many a warrior to their shamefaced rampages. Perhaps I will not chop off your head after all."

Frog tutted and sheathed his sword. "Yeah, well I wouldn't feel proper fighting a lady and a flobbily old fossil anyway," he said.

The woman bristled.

"Flobbily? Who's he talking about?" asked the man, picking cake out of his beard.

"By the six-and-a-half realms — I don't think this creature knows who we are," said the woman.

"Majesties!" came a cry. A dozen guards emerged from the treeline, dressed in battle-worn armour and wielding swords and shields. The foremost guard — red-faced and sporting a strikingly bushy moustache — added, "We heard, 'AAH!' and 'OOOH!' and—" he gasped at the sight of the stunned monster. "Grool's beard — it's a shyclops! Protect the King and Queen!"

"Yes, save us! Save us again!" shrieked the old man.

"You're too late, Captain Camperlash," said the woman. "This determined little gobbin did your job for you."

"He did? He did!" concurred the King, happily.

"I am not a gobbin," Frog began. "I'm a—
Wait, did he say, 'King and Queen'?"

"Mud-suckin' gobbin spewn! Shut
yer hole an' avert yer ogle!" growled
Captain Camperlash, his face redder than
bloodberries. He brandished his sword in
Frog's direction. "None may look upon the
Majesties without prior appointment!"

"Unclench, Captain," said the woman. "This creature clearly does not know that he is in the presence of the sovereign monarchs of Kingdomland."

"The wuh?" blurted Frog.

"Hello gobbin," she said, holding out her hand. "We are the King and Queen of Everything."

The Champion of Kingdomland

"*You're* the King and Queen?" Frog asked, inappropriately high-fiving the Queen.

"Are we?" blurted the King.

Frog peered at them through wide eyes, suddenly remembering a grand painting he'd seen two days ago in the royal palace – a portrait of the King and Queen of Everything. The noble, trim-bearded, shiny-crowned king in that picture looked nothing like this fat, crumb-faced old potato … but the resemblance of the woman to the copper-haired Queen suddenly struck him like a shyclops' club to the head.

It was them – Princess Rainbow's parents – the rulers of Kingdomland.

"Then you've *heard* of us, at least," the

Queen snorted. "I was beginning to suspect that you'd spent your whole life under a rock."

"Actually, it was a farty little island," Frog replied. "I'm trying to get back there. Do you know the way to the waterfall in the sky?" He pointed to the waterfall behind them. "Like that, but much, much, much, much, much, much, much bigger."

"You know, we could use a quick-thinking young warrior like you," said the Queen. "A great battle awaits the Royal Army of Everything. A just crusade against our sworn enemy. What say you? Would you pledge your sword to the one true cause? Could you be a champion of Kingdomland?"

"*Champion?*" blurted Captain Camperlash.

"Champion?" repeated Frog. He'd never considered it.

Things You Can Do If You Don't
Want to Be a Prince Anymoor

Expllorer
Arm Ressler
Dog trayner

"I left our current champion in the palace,
guarding the princess," the Queen continued.
"But Man Lor has taken one too many blows
to the head to be of any use on our crusades.
So, what do you say, Frog? Do you think
you've got what it takes?"

Frog rubbed his chin. Since he'd spent
most of his life thinking he was a royal
prince, becoming a royal champion would,
technically, be a demotion. But Buttercup had
always said he should be good – and what
could be more good than battling enemies
and being mighty on a day-to-day basis?

The big question, thought Frog. *This could be the answer!*

"But Majesty! A muck-eyed gobbin in the royal army?" growled Camperlash, shocking Frog out of his reverie. "They're soil-sacks, the lot of 'em! Did we not just spend the last month crushin' a gobbin rebellion in the Upside-Downtains?"

"For the last— I am *not* a gobbin! My name is Frog ... and my *nostrils* are mightier than you," began Frog. "I just defeated a whole shyclops while you were still tying up your bootlaces! Plus you should have seen all the mightiness I did at the royal palace! Just ask Princess Rainbow – I was—"

"What d'you know of Her Tremendously Royal Princess Rainbow, y' newt-suckin' unwash?" interrupted Camperlash. "An' what was you doin' at the royal palace?"

"I – I…" Frog bit his lip. It had been two days since he had saved Princess Rainbow and defeated the Kroakan invaders. But he had also accidentally brought about the destruction of the royal palace. Since he had just been offered the role of Kingdomland's champion, he thought it might be better not to tell the King and the Queen the whole truth. So, Frog did something he'd never done before.

He lied.

"I just … popped in for polished sandwiches, that's all," he said, awkwardly. "It was actually pretty uneventful…"

The Queen peered at Frog. The captain peered at Frog. Then:

"He's green like peas," the King interjected. "I like peas."

"That settles it then!" laughed the Queen.

"Frog, by the powers vested in me — by me — I hereby enlist you to the Royal Army of Everything."

"Great!" said Frog. "But first, I need to get back to the island. I need to get back to—"

"Frog," interrupted the Queen, as if she owned his name. "The King and Queen of Everything are requesting your aid. Whatever else you have to do, can it not wait until you have secured your legend as champion — perhaps even the greatest champion Kingdomland has ever known?"

Camperlash huffed loudly, but the Queen's words had already filled Frog's brain. Perhaps finding Buttercup *could* wait — just for a while. Perhaps she would be even more impressed that he was a mighty champion instead of a prince. A wide grin spread across Frog's face.

"That's what I thought," added the Queen. "Captain, give our young champion here a horse."

"You mean a steed? No need!" Frog cried. "Sheriff Explosion! Your master summons you!"

Frog gestured to the treeline. After a pause Sheriff Explosion emerged, chewing lazily on a flower.

"See?" said Frog, proudly.

"Baa," added the sheep.

The Royal Army

With his trusty steed in tow, Frog followed the King and Queen through the dusky-blue forest, a smile fixed to his face. Even the swarm of imp-O-lights that flitted around him, farting and burping in his ears, couldn't dampen his mood.

"I'm going to be the mightiest, most folk-saving champion ever," he said. "I don't know why I didn't think of it before. I'll do so much goodness I'll peace-up the whole world. BU-DOOSH! FWA-POW! KA-PEACE!"

"Baa," bleated Sheriff Explosion.

"Then straight after that," Frog added, "I'll go back to the island and get Butter—"

"I've got my eyes on you, y' crusted flem,"

47

hissed a tomato-cheeked Camperlash, peering down on Frog from his horse as they trotted past. "Y' think yer somethin' special, but the Queen's always doin' this – she goes through new champions like tomorrow ain't comin'. Why, even I was— Never mind." He trotted closer and snarled, "The King and Queen's my responsibility. Y' even look at 'em funny with them fat gobbin eyes and I'll gut you like a gulper, got it?"

"Pfff – weren't you paying attention? I'm the champion! Cham-pee-on," replied Frog, striding ahead into a large, circular clearing. "When did *you* last do something hero— Uuh?"

Even in the failing light of dusk, Frog could see dozens of armed and armoured royal warriors. They were gathered round campfires, feeding horses, sharpening swords and eating hearty portions of unfussy, unpolished sandwiches.

They looked like they were getting ready for a fight.

"Yoiks … you must have a million soldiers. Maybe even a hundred," Frog noted, dragging his steed along as he caught up with the King and Queen.

"Four hundred and two, at the last count," said the Queen. They made their way through the camp, soldiers peering suspiciously at the green stranger in their midst. "It is not easy being the King and Queen of Everything, Frog. We wish for the realms to exist together in peace. If they do not, we must *impose* peace upon them."

"Peas!" the King added. "It's easier if we all like peas…"

"But there are those who wish to sow

discord," the Queen continued, guiding
Frog and his sheep inside a large, tented area.
"They are the enemies of Kingdomland —
the enemies of peace."

Frog put his hands upon his hips.

"I'll make them want peace, just you
watch," he said. "I'm skilled-up like you
wouldn't believe."

AN IMPORTUNT LIST OF WHAT
MAKES FROG A CHAMPION

Mighty legs for jumping
Excellent strong mussuls
Most non-stoppabul by a million
Kroak Kloak for doing invisible
magic ninja things
Allways makes the rite choice
Good
Qwite handsum

The Queen took the deepest, longest breath of air Frog had ever seen.

"Tomorrow, we go to war," she said. She made her way over to a small banquet table, which was piled high with polished sandwiches and rim-full cups of runnymead. She handed one cup to Frog and another to the King. "But tonight, we honour our new champion. Make us proud, Frog."

"I'll champion like crazy! I'll make you so proud that even if all your hair fell out you wouldn't care," Frog assured them. He swigged the runnymead and fed his sheep a sandwich. In that moment, he felt better than he had in ages.

But a day later, Frog wished he'd never met the King and Queen of Everything.

The UnSlumber

That night, with his belly full of sandwiches and runnymead (and snuggled against the warm wool of his trusty steed) Frog slept more soundly than he had since leaving the island. Until:

"Turnips!"

Frog sat upright. The stale, burpish smell was unmistakable – Buttercup loved nothing more than boiling a freshly dug batch in the morning. Frog rubbed his eyes and looked around. The morning sun seeped in through threadbare curtains, picking out familiar shapes – the quill pen sitting in its pot … shelves of princely journals … the rock with a face drawn on it.

He was back in his bedroom, on the Island

at the Edge of the End of the World.

He was home.

"What the ... what?" Frog muttered, leaping out of bed. Sheriff Explosion was nowhere to be seen, nor the Queen, King or royal army. Frog hurried out of his bedroom and into the kitchen. Sure enough, standing with her back to him, stirring a simmering pot of turnips, was the plump, curly-haired figure of—

"Buttercup!" Frog cried. He ran over and gave her such a mighty hug that she gasped with laughter. "I missed you! And the World hasn't Ended! And I'm from outer space! And ... how am I here?"

"Oh, my dear Frog, I missed you so much..." Buttercup said, holding his face. Frog looked up at her – and his eyes grew wide.

"Uh, you have a moustache," Frog replied.

Buttercup reached up and felt the thick, dark hair on her top lip.

"So I do," she replied, stroking her moustache with a smile. "Fancy that."

"What's … going on?" uttered Frog, suddenly suspicious.

"You know, these things aren't half bad," said a bone-shaking rumble of a voice. Frog spun round to see the rarewolf, perched uncomfortably – impossibly – on a stool at the kitchen table. He was munching on a turnip. "Don't get me wrong, I'd rather eat a rain-deer, but as vegetables go, they have a rustic charm."

"Rarewolf! How did you get away from the mystery Kroakan? Is she still messing with your brain-juice? How did—" Frog froze, peering at the rarewolf. "*Wait a miniature…*

Is this a dream? This is a dream, isn't it…"

"Call it what you like," huffed the rarewolf. "It's nothing to do with me. I'm just a figment of your imagination. Like them."

Frog noticed the other chairs around the table were suddenly occupied. Princess Rainbow waved at him, and he saw that she had polished sandwiches instead of hands. Next to her sat the wizard, Oldasdust, who – despite being dead – crunched on a plateful of his own magical talismans.

"Ignore them, Frog. Only I am real," explained Buttercup. "Think of it as me visiting you in dreamland … a meeting of our conscious and subconscious minds. It is called the UnSlumber."

"Wuh?" replied Frog.

Buttercup added, "Apparently in the back of your mind I have facial hair."

"What the bumbles? How are you doing dream visits?" asked Frog. "You never did that on the island."

"I never had to — you were always there in the next room!" laughed Buttercup. She paused. "Frog, I hope you know I've always wanted the best for you."

"Yep, I know — you tried to save me from the End of the World!" replied Frog. "Except … except I just told you the World *hasn't* Ended … and you don't even seem surprised."

Buttercup returned to stirring turnips. "One day, I hope you'll forgive me," she said, finally. "I hope you'll understand that I was only trying to save you … from your destiny."

"Destiny? Destiny is bumdrops! Why is everyone so worried about it?" replied Frog.

"Anyway, you've got it backwards — you don't save me, I save you! You should have seen all the saving I did last week…"

Buttercup bowed her head, as if her thoughts were heavy.

"Frog, listen to me," she began. "When you left the island … the future began. There are things happening now that are out of everyone's control. You must be ready."

"Were you not listening?" replied Frog. "The End of the World alien space invasion is over! I stopped it."

Buttercup took Frog's hand and guided him to the back door.

"Did you?" she asked, opening the door.

Frog expected to see the back garden, with its burpy vegetable patch and lonely tree — and beyond, the calm waters of the Inbetween. What he saw was a vast expanse of outer space, a universe of darkness and stars, stretching out endlessly in every direction.

"Yoiks…" whispered Frog. He peered into the void. There, waiting, hovering in the ocean of space, were dozens of huge, oil-black, saucer-shaped objects — each as smooth as a pebble. A grating, blood-chilling hum filled the air.

"What are they?" whispered Frog.

"The future," replied Buttercup. "Run and hide, Frog — there's no shame in it. Run and hide."

"Run and hide?" repeated Frog. "I've never runned and hid in my— Yoiks!"

Frog saw the ground evaporate under his feet. He tried to hang on but Buttercup was gone … along with the rarewolf … the princess … the house … everything.

Frog fell into darkness, his scream swallowed by the vacuum of space.

AAAAAAAAAAAAAAaaaaaaaaaa...

The Valley of the Bragon

"Up! Up, y' sluggan snails!"

"AAAA— wuh?" groaned Frog, Captain Camperlash's cries waking him with a start. He opened his eyes to find Sheriff Explosion staring blankly back at him.

"Baa?" said his sheep. Frog's eyes darted around. He was back in the tent, freezing air biting at his fingers and toes.

"I just had the loop-de-doopiest dream — at least I think I did," he said, rubbing his temples. "Buttercup knew that the World hadn't Ended, and Princess Rainbow and the rarewolf were there, and all sorts. It was bonkers. Maybe I had too much runnymead last night..."

Frog shook off the dream and leaped out

of bed. He quickly pulled on his catastrophe pants and stepped outside.

"What the ... what?"

It was as if the world had been transformed overnight. A thick blanket of snow covered every field, forest, hill and mountain as far as

the eye could see.

Almost as impressive was the sight of the great royal army decamping and saddling up. Captain Camperlash was already on horseback, his face turning cherry red as he rallied the troops.

"Wits an' swords about you, armpits! Today we teach that tainted bragon who rules this land!"

"Bragon?" repeated Frog.

"An enemy of peace," said a voice. Frog spun round to see the Queen of Everything, clad head to toe in battle-worn golden armour. In her hands she held a pair of leather-bound boots lined with thick fur.

"Here, I brought you a gift," she said, handing them to Frog.

"Thanks!" he replied. "It *has* been a few days since I felt my toes."

"A champion cannot afford to get cold feet," the Queen said with a smile. "So, are you ready to show that bragon who's boss?"

"I'm the teacher — and I only teach defeat!" Frog replied, putting his hands on his hips. "Also, what's a bragon?"

The Bragon

The Queen says the bragon is
a full-on enemmy of Kingdomland. He's allways
boasting on abowt how grate he is even though
he's definitely not. Akshully he is really bad.
He has wings to way owt here and mad fangs
and crazed awfull stink breth and he does so
much badness that he neads to be stopped.
The Queen says he's dangeruss to ~~peas pease~~
peace in Kingdomland and that probubly only the
most skilled-up champion ever can defeat him.
Luckilee she knows one.

Frog closed his book. He pulled his cape
around him and stared at his new, deliciously
warm boots. He had been marching through
the snow for most of the day (his trusty
steed following behind) and had all but
forgotten his strange dream. Much mightier,

he thought, to focus on something real, being a bragon-defeating champion.

"Are we nearly there yet?" asked Frog for the eighty-third time. He looked up over the soldiers' heads and saw the sun start to dip below the horizon. As they made their way into a wide valley, large crimson-red mountains loomed large on either side, glinting like quartz where the snow had not settled. At the base of the mountains, cavernous openings in the rock led into shadowy tunnels.

The army was halfway through the valley when Frog saw Captain Camperlash stop his horse and raise a fist high into the air. The army ground to a halt. There was a long, tense silence, then:

"Bragon!"

At the captain's cry, Frog looked up. From atop the mountain emerged the shape of the bragon. The beast plummeted from the sky, opening its huge wings wide and swooping over the royal army, spooking horses and causing the less courageous soldiers to duck.

Finally, the bragon dived towards the ground, stopping in mid-air and landing no more than ten paces from the King and Queen.

"Yoiks…" whispered Frog. The barrel-chested bragon was even taller than the rarewolf. Its scaly hide was a rich, reddish colour, and its wings were striped in an array of bright blues, greens and yellows. Atop its head was an impressive plume of purple hair, which it flicked proudly as it landed.

"Behold the enemy of Kingdomland," hissed the Queen to Frog. "Captain!"

"Bragon! Villain! Foul, lie-mouthed spewn!" snarled Camperlash, turning redder than roseberries. "Kneel before the King and Queen of Every—"

"Face the Champion of Kingdomland!"

interrupted Frog. He hopped on to Sheriff Explosion and gave him a sharp nudge in the haunches. The sheep was so startled it actually started running, bolting past Captain Camperlash.

"Stink-pus gobbin! Get back 'ere!" the captain hissed.

"It appears our new champion hungers for battle," noted the Queen as Frog raced towards the bragon on his trusty steed.

"Why is that gobbin riding a cloud?" asked the King.

The Duke

"Onward, Sheriff Explosion!" cried Frog, delighted that his steed was actually being trusty for once.

It did not last. At the sight of the bragon, Sheriff Explosion skidded to a halt, sending Frog flying over his head and into the snow.

"Baa," said the sheep, sheepishly.

Frog quickly scrambled to his feet and drew his sword.

"Bragon, face me! I am Frog, the mightiest champion of Kingdomland ever!"

The bragon raised an eyebrow.

"Welcome, Frog, to you and yours!" he boomed. He flicked his purple quiff and pointed to himself with his thumb claws. "You probably already know … the Duke."

"Duke? Duke Shmook!" Frog replied. "All I need to know is, you're bad … and beating badness is my specialist subject. Prepare to chew the gum of defeat!"

"Of course you know the Duke! Everyone knows the Duke!" cried the bragon, his voice resounding through the valley. "For the Duke's legend is known from Terra Further to the Forgotten Sands! The Duke is so much bragon that one name cannot contain him! You stand before The Wondrous Thundersnort, Oval the Uncornerable, That Unpausing Comma, Tantamountian Truthpumper, Falderal O'Blarney … you stand before Duke Bombastion the Many-Named!"

"Who?" asked Frog.

"You only have to look at the Duke to know how tall-headed and strong-winged and flower-smelling he is," continued the bragon, visibly swelling with pride. "But there's more! The Duke is so strong that he could throw his mum over the moon! The Duke has more mightiness in his sneeze than you could ever dream about, even in those really good dreams where you've got all your clothes on and no one's chasing you."

"Pfff... Says you," tutted Frog. "I'm mightier by a million – you should have seen all the—"

"The Duke is so mighty that if you looked up 'mightiness' in the dictionary, the Duke would appear behind you and pull your pants over your head," interrupted the bragon loudly. He was expanding like a balloon.

"I've got mightiness coming out of my ears!" said Frog, waving Basil Rathbone.

"You don't even have a sword or—"

"The Duke is so mighty that if he farted, it would change the smell of the world," boomed the bragon.

"Now you're just being—" Frog began.

"The Duke is so mighty that he could drink a volcano!"

"That's bonkers. No one can—"

"The Duke is so mighty that the next mightiest thing after the Duke is still the Duke!"

"Stop boasting! You're not even—"

"The Duke is so mighty that he could rule the whole of Kingdomland if he wanted!" said the bragon, by now so swollen that he looked as if he might pop. "And the Duke would be a better ruler than the King and Queen of Everything!"

A gasp rang out from the royal army and

echoed into the valley.

"Canker-mouthed article! Y' dare set yerself above the Majesties?" roared Camperlash, his face exploding with redness. "Seize him!"

"Consider him— Hey!" began Frog. The bragon had begun to float up into the air. "Get back here! I have to bop your chops!"

"Can't be helped," said the bragon, with a flick of his hair and a flash of sharp teeth. "The Duke must fly!"

"Stop! I haven't defeated you yet!" cried Frog, springing upwards on his mighty legs. He grabbed the bragon by a claw as it launched itself ever higher.

"Grabby gobbin, the Duke is too handsome to be manhandled," laughed the bragon. "Let's go for a ride!"

"Wai— AAH!" cried Frog, his stomach

churning as they corkscrewed in the air, the bragon's booming laughter filling the valley. Frog had no idea what was up or down. He caught sight of the royal army and accidentally kicked a few soldiers in the head as the bragon soared above them.

"Sorry! 'Scuse me! Champion coming through!" he cried.

"Archers, bring down the beast!" hollered Camperlash.

Frog heard the Queen yell, "Hold fire! Let's see what our champion can do!" and breathed a short-lived sigh of relief.

A moment later, the bragon swept upwards and towards the mountain. "The Duke can do this all day!" it cried.

"So can I!" replied Frog, trying not to be sick. "This is noth— AAAAH!"

He saw the jagged mountainside rush towards him. The bragon pulled up at the last moment and Frog was buffeted against the rock face with a THUD ("Ow!") THUD ("Ow!") THUD ("Ow!") THUD!

A dazed Frog felt one of his hands slip as the bragon looped the loop. In a moment

he would fall to his doom. He grabbed his
sunder-gun from his holster and – his head
spinning – opened fire.

"YooooOOOOoooW!" the bragon cried,
as a green beam of energy seared through
his wing. He immediately spiralled out
of control. Frog saw mountain … sky …
mountain … sky … ground. The bragon
landed hard, bouncing and careering along
the sun-dried earth until he skidded to a halt
at the feet of the King and Queen.

"The sky is falling!" howled the King.
"Every monarch for themselves!"

"Frog!" cried the Queen.

"All … in a day's … championing,"
groaned Frog, crawling out from underneath
the bragon. He struggled to his feet as Sheriff
Explosion nuzzled his leg in relief.

"Ha! They will sing songs about you,

Frog," laughed the Queen. "We brought a whole army to defeat the bragon and you managed it single-handed! The final honour must be yours and yours alone."

"Final honour?" repeated Frog, rubbing his head.

"The honour of imposing peace, of course," said the Queen with a smile. "Be a champion … and slay the bragon."

The Slaying

"Slay?" blurted Frog, holding the Queen's sword in both hands. "As in, *slay* slay?"

"Of course," replied the Queen. "Draw your sword and cut off the bragon's head."

"Chop chop," added the King with a sigh.

"Yeah, but, I mean … the bragon's *bad*, right?" said Frog, his hand hovering over his scabbard. "I mean, really bad – burning villages and eating old ladies and shouting at kittens…?"

"Lily-gut! Y' heard the bragon – he said he was better than the King and Queen," snarled Camperlash, his moustache hair standing on end. "Head-chopping's the least he deserves!"

"Wait, that's it?" said Frog. "You want to

slay him for what he said? That's bumdrops! You said he was an enemy of Kingdomland. I can't slay his whole business just 'cause of talking."

"Baa," said Sheriff Explosion, possibly in agreement.

"Why not?" asked the Queen. "If anyone could claim to be the greatest, how would we know who actually *was* the greatest? How would we decide who should be King or Queen? It is only by agreement that we can have peace in Kingdomland."

"But everyone knows who you are — you have the shined-up crowns and the loyal subjects," exclaimed Frog.

"Do y' duty, slack-wit!" yelled Camperlash. "Slay the beast before it stirs!"

"You can't go around slaying folk just for

saying stuff," Frog said. "It isn't good. "

"Frog," said the Queen, firmly. "Do as I command. Slay the bragon."

"No!" Frog said.

A gasp rang out from the royal army.

"'No'?" said the King, trying it out. "I'm not sure I know this word. What does it mean?"

"I am your Queen," said the Queen through gritted teeth. "You will do as I command or – champion or no champion – I will cut off your head."

Frog looked back at the army ... at Camperlash ... at the King and Queen. Then he rolled his neck until it cracked, and drew his sword.

"Actually, you're not my Queen," he said. "I'm an alien prince from outer space, so I don't have to do what you say at all.

Which means I'm not slaying this bragon –
and no one else is slaying him either."

The Escape

"I'm not sure I quite understand this new champion of ours," noted the King of Everything, as Frog put himself between the wounded bragon and the royal army. "Isn't he meant to do as he's told?"

"Y' dare defy their Majesties? Y' dare call yourself a prince?" barked Camperlash, his face redder than rubyfruit. "Crusted flem! Inconstant betrayal monkey!"

Frog saw a flash of steel as Camperlash unsheathed his sword. He drew Basil Rathbone and waved it wildly.

"Get back, all of you! I'm two seconds away from going full mighty!" he cried, Sheriff Explosion cowering behind him.

"It appears the enemies of Kingdomland

are everywhere — even in our own ranks," began the Queen. "A shame — I had high hopes for you, Frog,"

"Bumdrops! I am not an enemy of Kingdomland!" he insisted. "I'm an enemy of slaying!"

"Enough," added the Queen, coolly. "Throw down your weapons and surrender, or my archers will drop you where you stand."

Frog heard the creak of bowstrings and saw a dozen arrows aiming at his head.

"Try it!" he bellowed. "You'll all get a slice of the mightiness pie!"

"Time t' die, gobbin," hissed Camperlash. WHiiiiiiSHT – SHUNK!

Before he could flinch, Frog saw an arrow strike the ground inches from the Queen of Everything's feet. The royal archers looked confused. Frog turned and looked up. Atop an outcropping of rock was the now-familiar sight of the rarewolf and the mystery Kroakan.

"A rarewolf?" whimpered the King. "It's the End of the World!"

"It cannot be… We destroyed them all…" whispered the Queen.

The rarewolf gave a long, loud howl and cried, "I live, O Queen! I live until you kill me!"

"What the bumbles is he on about? The mystery Kroakan's evil psychic space eye messed up his brain-juice something proper," Frog whispered to Sheriff Explosion. He watched the rarewolf leap into the valley and away, the Kroakan holding tightly to its mane of fur.

"A lifetime of polished sandwiches to

whoever brings me that rarewolf!" bellowed the Queen, as she mounted her horse. "Captain, you and your squadron guard the prisoners! If they try to escape... Well, you know the rest."

"Chop chop," added the King, helpfully.

Frog watched the army move swiftly off, a sea of soldiers and horses pounding through the snow after their prey. He and Sheriff Explosion backed towards the bragon as Camperlash and half a dozen soldiers encircled them.

"Uh ... are you all right?" Frog asked the bragon.

"You ... punctured me!" he replied, flexing his damaged wing.

"I'm sorry! I thought you were bad! I didn't know they wanted to kill you just for talking bumdrops," said an embarrassed

Frog. "Anyway, I was just about to fight the whole, entire army to save you, so..."

"Save me? As in, the *opposite* of kill me?" said the bragon, doubtfully.

"Well, yep," replied Frog. "I'm anti slaying — my champion business is strictly heroic."

"Baa," added Sheriff Explosion, helpfully.

"Well, in that case, one bad turn immediately followed by one good turn deserves another good turn," the Duke said, getting to his feet.

"Wuh?" replied Frog.

"Shut yer vocal-holes, y' false-tongued worms of untruth!" hissed Camperlash, brandishing his sword. "I'm goin' to slay y' both, here an' now, and be done with it."

"Bring it on!" Frog began. "I'll—"

"The Duke could not be slain with all the slaying swords in Kingdomland!" interrupted the bragon — and then began to swell. "The Duke's left buttock is as mighty as a hundred royal champions. A single feather on the Duke's wings could beat sense into the whole kingdom! And the only reason the Duke said he was greater than the King and Queen ... is because the Duke is greater!"

"False-head!" roared Camperlash. He raised his sword as the bragon swelled even further...

"The Duke's greatness cannot be helped! The Duke could out-rule the King and Queen with one wing tied behind his back!" the bragon replied, swollen to bursting. "Now ... the Duke must fly!"

The bragon grabbed Frog by the cape (and Sheriff Explosion by his leg) and immediately began floating into the air.

Camperlash swung his longsword at them,

but the bragon was already too high.

"Spit-outs! Get back 'ere!" roared Camperlash.

"Wait!" cried Frog. "I'm still defeating them!"

"He that boasts and runs away," replied the bragon. "Lives to boast from a safe distance."

The House in the Clouds

The bragon floated up and up, the soldiers and the snow-covered valley shrinking below them along with the sound of Camperlash's insults. As Sheriff Explosion bleated with terror, Frog glanced up at the bragon, who was doing his best to steer them with only one good wing.

"Put me down! I was just about to bake the doughnut of defeat and use them all as the filling!" protested Frog.

"The Duke could have defeated them in the middle of an afternoon nap!" replied the bragon, as they became engulfed by low-lying clouds. "The Duke could have defeated them in a dream and then woken up to find he had defeated them in real life! The Duke could have— Oh, wait, we're here."

"Here where?" asked Frog.

A moment later, they emerged through the clouds. The light from the setting sun blinded Frog for a moment, but as his vision cleared, he spotted something in the sky. Before them, suspended in the air, was a house.

"What the ... what?" said Frog.

As the bragon floated towards it, Frog could see that the house was constructed from fine, sky-blue stone, and looked as steady as if built upon foundations — even with nothing but nothingness beneath it.

"Welcome to the *Omnium Gatherum* – my humble home," said the bragon, his voice suddenly thin and unimposing. He dropped Frog and Sheriff Explosion carefully onto the porch before landing. He opened the front door and was about to step through when he looked down at his still-swollen body. "Silly me – hang on a tinkle…"

BUU-U-RRRRRP!

The bragon let out an almighty belch.

Frog looked back to see that he'd returned to his pre-swollen state. "Begging your pardon. After you, gentlefolk," he added in a reedy, nasal voice.

Frog led Sheriff Explosion inside, who bleated with relief at having something solid beneath his hooves. The front room of the house was simply decorated in various blues. It was filled with an unfussy collection of blue furniture, including a blue table upon which sat a blue teapot and cups. In the centre of the room stood a free-standing blue door that led nowhere at all. The room was otherwise empty but for a collection of twenty or so blue boxes, stacked in neat piles against the far wall. The boxes rattled and hummed with enchantment, as if barely able to contain the objects inside.

"This place is bonkers," said Frog. "How does it stay up?"

"Mostly magic, I think," replied the bragon, retrieving a pair of spectacles from the table and putting them on. He pointed to a large wooden lever protruding from the floor at the base of the largest window. "But I know better than to meddle with the machinery of a magical house, by gosh.

Truth be told, I won this place in a card game with an old wizard possessed of an unfeasibly long moustache and an impractically tall hat."

"Oldasdust?" asked Frog.

"Well, he was certainly past his prime," laughed the bragon. "Have you seen him of late? How is he?"

"Sort of dead," answered Frog sadly. "But that wizard kind of dead where they go plooooooof! And then they're just not here any more."

"Oh, poo. He was a nice fellow – for a wizard," said the bragon. "Still, having his collection of magical whatsits and thingamajingles has its uses."

"What do you mean?" asked Frog.

"I'll show you. Open that box next to you," the bragon replied. "Find me a stone with a helping hand carved on the front."

Frog opened the box and peered inside. It was brimming with dozens of small stone talismans, each with a symbol carved upon it.

"These are Oldasdust's wizard things! For all his – EXPOOM! – magical business," he said, rootling through the box. "Yoiks … there's enough stuff in these boxes for a whizz-banging *army* of wizards."

Frog found a stone with a hand carved on it and tossed it to the bragon.

"I'm still trying to work out what they all do, truth be told," said the bragon. He crushed the stone over his wing and it dissolved into a bright sprinkling dust. The wound immediately began to heal. The bragon smiled and added, "See? Take one – you might need it with the enemies you made today…"

"Pfff — those grotty head-choppers don't scare me," huffed Frog. He picked out a stone with two circles — one large, and one small — carved upon it, and slipped it into his pocket. Then he pointed to the door in the middle of the room. "What's that for?"

"Who knows?" replied the bragon, pressing his spectacles on to his nose. "The only thing the wizard made me promise was that I never open that door."

"But it doesn't even go anywhere," Frog muttered, as he walked around it. The door was chained shut. On it were written the words:

ENTER NOT
UPON PAIN OF A
WIZARD'S WITHERING STARE!

ENTER
NOT
UPON PAIN OF
A WIZARD'S
WITHERING STARE !!

"Just more wizard weirdness," chuckled the bragon. "Still, I didn't mind honouring his request – I felt bad taking this place off his hands, since I'm a such terrible card player by bragon standards…"

"Wait…" began Frog. "That actually sounded like … like whatever the *opposite* of boasting is."

"Me boast?" replied the bragon. "What

97

about you? All that 'I'm so mighty!' and 'I was about to bake the doughnut of defeat' and 'You'll get all the pie!' nonsense? At least I put my hot air to good use..."

"Yeah, but all that's true! I'm— Wait, 'hot air'?" repeated Frog.

"The bragon's gift," replied the bragon. "The more I boast, the more hot air I have to carry me into the clouds, by gosh! Without hot air a bragon can only glide ... with it he can *fly*."

Frog slapped his forehead.

"So, that's what all that 'I'm the Duke' bumdrops was about?"

"It's all flimflam for flight's sake! My real name is Nigel," said the bragon. He made his way over to a small table and picked up a blue teapot in his claws. "Bragons live to fly... Once you have soared through the air, you realize that life on the ground is a load of old smell. But it's a lonely life. We bragons got so sick of listening to each other toot our own trumpets that we chose to live at different corners of Kingdomland. I haven't seen the others in years, truth be told…"

"So, why don't you just do your boasting in private?" Frog asked.

The bragon poured blue tea into two blue china cups and let out a long sigh. "Bragons are cursed with cruel magic. The hot air only fills us if someone is around to hear our boasts." He handed a cup of tea to Frog, who followed him over to a window. They stuck out their heads and looked down. "That's why I love it up here. Before I won this house, mine was a dank existence in the caves beneath the mountains. It was so hard to know where to wait for passers-by. And then there were the mice-lice, always trying to drink my tea… But up here, I can see the whole valley — and swoop down on whomever I please."

Frog peered down into the valley. Through the encroaching darkness he could see the King and Queen's forces — looking not much bigger than ants — tramping through the snow.

"As long as you don't swoop down on them again," Frog said.

"Baa," agreed Sheriff Explosion.

"Sound advice, by gosh," nodded the bragon, his claw around his own throat. "Flying can be tricky with your head chopped—"

"Wait, we *have* to swoop down on them!"

interrupted Frog. "We have to swoop down there *right now!*"

"What?" began the bragon. "But you just said—"

"They caught him! They caught the rarewolf!" Frog cried, pointing to the back of the royal convoy. A dozen soldiers dragged the bound, motionless rarewolf through the snow, with the mystery Kroakan tethered behind him. "Why doesn't the rarewolf use his thundering and lightninging?" muttered Frog. "He should be able to out-mighty the army almost as easily as me."

"Oh, I expect it'll be fine ..." said the bragon unconvincingly. He sipped his tea and added, "I'm sure everyone's put the whole human–rarewolf war behind them..."

"Human—rarewolf *war*?" cried Frog. "Oh, great! The rarewolf's going to be sliced up for polished sandwiches! You have to fly me down there, bragon!"

"No chance!" protested the bragon. "I'm not going anywhere near them, due to the aforementioned head-chopping."

"The rarewolf tried to help us. Now we have to help him!" cried Frog. "Look, I am a mighty alien outer space someone from the planet Kroak and I command you to fly me down there!"

"Now hang on a tinkle," began the bragon. "A) I have no idea what you just said, and B) I am not swooping down there to face certain death. Even if I was filled with hot air there's no way I could carry that great beast to safety. Meanwhile, you'd have to take on the whole army single-handed and despite what you think, you wouldn't last two minutes."

"I'd last a million minutes!" cried Frog.

"You've only seen me at twelve-per-cent mightiness! I'll save the rarewolf and protect you – trust me!"

"I'm not staking my life on a hollow boast," insisted the bragon. "I'd rather be a living coward than a dead hero."

"But they're going to kill him!" growled Frog.

"Better him than me!" replied the bragon. "No, I'm sorry, Frog – you don't need a bragon ... you need a miracle."

KNOCK.

KNOCK.

KNOCK.

Frog, the bragon and Sherriff Explosion turned slowly.

The knocking was coming from behind the door to nowhere.

"What the ... what?" muttered Frog.

CHAPTER TEN OR
THIRTEEN

The Door to Nowhere

KNOCK.

KNOCK.

KNOCK-KNOCK-KNOCK-KNOCK-KNOCK-KNOCK!

"Well, it's never done that before," whispered the bragon, inspecting the door to nowhere from both sides.

"Baa," said Sheriff Explosion.

Frog strode towards the door. "Whatever's knocking, it's going to knock the door *down* if we don't open it," he said. "Stand back ... this is a job for Basil Rathbone."

Frog drew his invincible sword and slashed the door's iron chains. They clattered to the ground in pieces. Frog took a breath, turned the handle and pulled open the door...

"See? I told you someone was home," said a tiny mouse of a voice.

Standing in the doorway, clad in a glittering golden dress, was the daughter of the King and Queen of Everything…

"Princess Rainbow?" blurted Frog.

"Hello, Greeny!" exclaimed the princess. "You look rubbish. What are you doing in the blue house?"

"What are *you* doing in the blue house?" Frog scoffed. "This door only goes to nowhere!"

"Oh, good, you're being silly again," the princess replied. "You being silly is my favourite thing."

She *klik-klakked* into the room on tiny heels. Frog tutted and peered inside the doorway. He was confronted by a pair of moderately thick tree trunks, which he quickly realized were legs. He looked up to see the brawny, furry-panted form of Princess Rainbow's bodyguard (and sometime royal champion), Man-Lor.

"I am Man-Lor," the barbarian boomed.

"I know who you are, you big lump of lumps," replied Frog, prodding one of the barbarian's bemuscled legs as he squeezed himself through the door. "But where did you come from?"

"The palace, silly Frog," replied Princess Rainbow. "This is the wizard's secret blue house in the clouds. It's where he kept all his secret magic things … except I knew about them because I made him tell me his secrets and he had to because I'm a princess." She pointed an outstretched finger at the bragon. "Who are you and what are you doing here?"

"This is Nigel the bragon," said Frog impatiently. "And we're actually in the middle of something important, so—"

"Well, I came to pay my respeks … after I tried on all my tiaras and rode all my new newnicorns," said the princess. "I came to put this where it belonged."

She nodded to Man-Lor. From behind his back, the barbarian produced a long, pointy wizard's hat and handed it to the princess.

"Oldasdust's Omen hat?" said Frog. "Uh, could you do this later? We're busy with—"

"Shh, quiet for the respeks," said the princess. She walked over to the blue table and placed the hat upon it. "Bye, old wizard of Kin'domland."

Princess Rainbow was silent for a long, reflective moment ... before clapping her hands together and jumping up and down.

"Respeks over! Let's play!"

"Play-shmay!" snapped Frog. "The rarewolf is about to get his head chopped off by the King and Queen of Everything!"

"Mummy and Daddy are here?" said the princess, looking around. "I want to see them! Where are they?"

"Down there," replied Frog, glaring at the bragon. "They're going to chop off the rarewolf's head and *someone* won't even fly me down— *Wait a mint* ... this is perfect!"

"Baa?" asked Sheriff Explosion.

"Don't you get it, bragon?" continued Frog. "Princess Rainbow is the King and Queen's daughter. The royal army isn't going to go anywhere near you if you're with her. While I'm doing my rescue business, the princess can stay with you and make sure no one chops your head off!"

"That might work," mused the bragon, adjusting his spectacles. "But couldn't the princess just tell the King and Queen not to chop off the rarewolf's head?"

"If there's a rarewolf down there, nothing will stop Mummy chopping its head off," replied the princess, peering down. "She hates rarewolves more than anything."

"I'll stop her with mightiness!" insisted

Frog. "Please, Nigel, you have to help me! The princess will protect you – right, Princess?"

"I want to see Mummy and Daddy!" she said.

"See?" said Frog. "So what do you say?"

The bragon swigged the last of his tea and swallowed nervously.

"I hope you're as mighty as you say you are, Frog."

Frog grinned. "I'm *mighterier*."

The Rescue

Nigel the bragon stood on the porch of the blue house, booming his best boasts. By the time he cried, "The Duke is more dazzlingly daring than a dozen derring-doers!" he looked fit to burst.

"Why does he sound funny?" asked Princess Rainbow. "And what's a 'dook'?"

"The Duke is … is…" the bragon added, peering down down at the royal army. "Is it too late to change my mind?"

"Yes!" replied Frog, scooping up Sheriff Explosion in both arms. "Everyone comes – the princess will make sure no one gets anything chopped off."

So the bragon took Man-Lor's hand, who took the hand of Princess Rainbow, who held out her hand for Frog.

"Uh…" said Frog, trying to free up a hand without dropping his trusty steed. Finally he shrugged and stuck out a leg. "Grab hold, Princess!"

In the valley below, the army had gathered in preparation for the execution. The rarewolf struggled against thick chains, its snout muzzled with leather straps. The Queen of Everything loomed over him and drew her sword.

"Oh dear," muttered the King. "Chop chop…"

"Please stop!" cried the mystery Kroakan, Captain Camperlash's blade at her throat. "The rarewolf is not your enemy – he would never have harmed the princess. He was after the egg – the golden egg!"

"Shut it, gobbin spewn!" snarled Camperlash, striking the Kroakan with the hilt of his sword. "You'll get yours for fraternizin' with an enemy of Kingdomland…"

"I swore that you would pay for invading my castle and threatening my daughter, rarewolf," said the Queen, holding her sword aloft. "I swore that all rarewolves would—"

BUURRRRRRP!

Everyone looked round to see who was responsible for the belch. Everyone except for the King, who looked up.

"I say, is that a bragon carrying a barbarian carrying a princess carrying a gobbin … carrying a cloud? It's the first sign of the End of the World!"

"Hands off that rarewolf!" came a cry.

This time the Queen looked up to see Frog dangling upside down – the final link in a bizarre, belching-bragon-propelled daisy chain. As the bragon swooped low he dropped Frog into the snow.

"Here is the champion!" cried Frog, scrambling to his feet. He struck a heroic pose as an upturned Sheriff Explosion flailed beside him. The Queen watched the bragon-chain wheel around to land further down the valley. Her eyes narrowed as she spotted her daughter slide down Man-Lor's back into the snow.

"Rainbow...? They have Rainbow!" she cried, lowering her sword. "Frog, if you so much as harm a hair on her head...!"

"The princess is fine – this is between you and me, Queen," boomed Frog, drawing his sword. "And the King, obviously. And the rarewolf, 'cause that's who I'm rescuing. And the mystery Kroakan. Actually I'm not really sure about her, but that doesn't mean you can chop off her head. And basically your whole, entire army. I hope you're all hungry 'cause the quiche of defeat is hot out of the oven!"

"Turncoatin' slope! I should have killed you when I had the chance," roared Camperlash.

"Stay your sword, Captain, I shall handle this," said the Queen. She strode through the snow towards Frog. When there were no more than five paces between them, she raised her sword and added, "Champions ... always spoiling for a fight."

"Wait, you want me to fight *you*? I can't do fighting with a Queen," Frog blurted. "Send someone else – you've got a whole army back there…"

"You *will* fight me!" roared the Queen, swinging her sword. Frog had no time for a skilful parry – with a forceful KLUNG of blade upon blade, he was flung backwards. The Queen wasted no time in attacking again. Frog felt KLUNG after KLUNG rattle his teeth and bones. He tried to dig his feet into the soft snow as he was driven back…

"Where is your might now, 'Champion'?" roared the Queen. Her blade was so swift that Frog barely saw it coming – it knocked Basil Rathbone from his hand and sent it flying into the snow.

He instinctively drew his sunder-gun but that too was slashed from his hand. A moment later, the Queen cast her own sword to the ground. Frog paused for a moment, not sure what to do next.

"Well? Fight!" the Queen cried.

Frog held his breath to activate his camouflage but the Queen was too fast for him — she brought her fist flying into his face.

THOMP!

Frog saw stars. There came another blow — and another — blow after blow until he found himself face down in the snow.

"Wuh the … Wuuh?" groaned Frog, his head spinning. He heard footsteps crunch through the snow, and the voice of the Queen.

"I have a seen a dozen champions come and go, Frog," she said. "They were all seduced by their own legend. They thought that their might was a gift that no one could take from them. But might … strength … power … these are crops to be tended."

Through swollen, half-opened eyes, Frog

saw the Queen retrieve her sword from the ground. Then he saw his own sword, lying in the snow at arm's length. With his last ounce of strength, he reached out…

"You could have been a great champion, Frog," said the Queen, holding her sword aloft. "Now you will be less than nothing – not so much as a footnote in history. Whereas I … I *am* Kingdomland."

Finally, Frog felt Basil Rathbone's handle. He wrapped his fingers around it and gripped tightly, but found he had no strength to lift it. As he slipped into unconsciousness, he heard the Queen cry, "Avert your eyes, Rainbow!" Then another noise – a grating hum, growing louder, filling the air…

Then darkness.

The Wake Up Call

"Frog?"

Frog opened his eyes. He checked that he still had a head, and sat up. He was on a small, wooden raft, floating across a vast expanse of water. It was the same crudely bound collection of logs he'd used to journey beyond his island home. But that raft had been smashed to pieces – he'd seen it happen.

Frog watched a whistle-fish bob out of the water, wink at him, and dive back into the deep.

"What th—" he began.

"I forgot how lovely the Inbetween is," said a soft voice. Frog turned to see Buttercup sitting at the other end of the raft, her feet dangling in the water as she stared out to sea.

"Buttercup?" said Frog. "How did I get here? I was in the valley. I was ... *wait a miniscule*, am I dreaming again? Am I UnSlumbering?"

"You tell me," said Buttercup, turning to him. While she still had her mass of brown hair, Buttercup had the face of a sheep.

"Yoiks!" said Frog. "Definitely UnSlumbering. But why am I asleep? I was in the valley..."

"You're unconscious, Frog. You're in a bit of a bad way, to be honest..." explained Buttercup. "But you're also in grave danger. I need you to wake up. Now."

"The Queen," said Frog, remembering. "She ... defeated me."

"Yes, I'm afraid she did. But that doesn't matter now," Buttercup replied.

"How does a champion get defeated by

the person who made him a champion in the first place?" continued Frog, peering down at his small, green hands. "I'm supposed to be mighty…"

"Frog, You have to wake up now," insisted Buttercup. "If you don't, you're going to die."

"Wake up? I don't know how," Frog replied.

Buttercup stood up and walked towards him. "A sharp shock should do it," she said.

"You have the face of a sheep," Frog replied. "That's pretty shocking."

Buttercup glanced at her reflection in the water and scratched her woolly chin. "You are the master of your destiny, whatever anyone else tries to tell you," she said, turning back to Frog. "And … I'm sorry about this."

"About what?" asked Frog. Then Buttercup pushed him as hard as she could.

"WuuAAA—?"

SPOSH.

The Second Wave

"—AuUH!" cried Frog, gasping for breath. He opened his swollen, bleary eyes…

"Wake up, Frog! Get up!"

Frog tried to move, but every last inch of him ached with pain. He realized he was back in the valley, lying in the snow — and with his head thankfully still attached to his body. But something had changed. His throat burned with an acrid taste. Cries and screams filled the air.

"What the … what?" he groaned, sitting up. He blinked twice, not quite able to believe what he was seeing.

The valley was on fire.

The blaze raged in all directions, burning even in the thick snow. The sky churned with

black smoke and whole mountains seemed to
have disappeared or crumbled into the valley.
Boulders crashed around him as whinnying,
riderless horses stampeded past. The Queen
of Everything was nowhere to be seen.

"Frog! Get up!" said a voice through the
din. "Get up, now!"

"Where ... Sheriff Explosion ... bragon?" Frog muttered. Through a fog of pain, he dragged himself to his feet. He limped aimlessly as screaming soldiers barged past him in the hope of escaping the bedlam.

"The sky falls!"

"It's the End of the World!"

"Tell my horse I love him!"

Through the smoke, Frog made out a large, dark shape — the rarewolf, still chained and muzzled. Next to him lay the mystery Kroakan, bound with ropes, crying out to him through the cacophony.

"Run, Frog! Find cover! They'll be back any second!"

"Back…? Who?" Frog mumbled, his head still ringing as he reached them. He looked down to see his magical sword, Basil Rathbone, still clutched in his hand. "Rescue … rarewolf…"

"No!" the mystery Kroakan cried. "Save yourself! Before they come— Oh *no*."

Frog heard the same grating hum he had heard when the Queen prepared to behead him … the sound he had heard in his dream. He turned slowly and looked up.

"Yoiks…" he muttered.

A dozen huge, curved, oil-black shapes appeared through the plumes of smoke. They soared through the valley faster than any bird or bragon — vast, polished pebbles, each thirty paces across and shimmering with energy.

"Kroakans…?" whispered Frog, gripping his sword weakly.

"Traceships! They won't stop until the valley is destroyed!" cried the mystery Kroakan. "Run!"

Frog saw wheeling, spinning ships dive towards them. A metallic shriek cut through the air as bright-green sunder-beams streaked towards the ground. The beams disintegrated everything they touched — soldiers, horses, trees — or burned great, fiery trenches into the earth.

"Look out!" yelled the mystery Kroakan.

"Yoiks!" Frog cried again, ducking as the traceships roared overhead. He turned back to the rarewolf and the mystery Kroakan and slashed at their bonds with his sword, freeing them in moments. The rarewolf got to its feet and shook ash and rubble from its back.

"Get on!" growled the rarewolf.

"No! Have ... to save ... Sheriff Princess ... Nigel Explosion..." muttered Frog.

"It's too late for that!" cried the mystery Kroakan. She grabbed Frog by the arm and leaped on to the rarewolf's back. "Rarewolf, cover us! Bring the lightning!"

"You know I can't do anything with all this snow everywhere!" roared the great, grey beast, as he sped across the burning valley. "Blasted stuff renders me powerless!"

"Then make for the caves!" replied the mystery Kroakan, pointing at a dark opening at the base of one of the mountains.

The rarewolf darted left, dodging sunder-beams and falling rubble and weaving past a tree that exploded into splinters. As he leaped for the cave, an overhead traceship unleashed a volley of sunder-beams. The ground beneath the rarewolf's feet exploded — and he, the mystery Kroakan and Frog were flung through the air...

The Cave

"OO-Oof!"

"YURPthhh!"

"GroOOosh!"

Frog lay on the cold, frozen ground, trying to work out which part of him hurt most. The force of the explosion had sent them flying into the cave.

"Up!" cried the mystery Kroakan, pulling Frog to his feet as sunder-beams rained down outside.

"Have to go back ... save sheep..." he muttered.

"If you die out there, your friends are doomed anyway!" the mystery Kroakan snapped. "Now, keep moving! Deeper into the cave!"

Frog was too weak to stop himself from being dragged through the narrow, dark tunnel that stretched deep into the mountain. The tunnel walls were coated in glowing, blue nectar, which illuminated the way ahead.

"What's — oww — happening?" Frog began, wincing with pain as the mystery Kroakan pulled him through the tunnels. "I ... was fighting the Queen..."

"That mad witch was about to chop off your head," grunted the rarewolf. "But the invaders interrupted. They put paid to her plan — and her army. Maybe they're not so bad after all!"

"But I thought I defeated all the Kroakans," said Frog. He added with a sigh, "I can't defeat anything..."

"You *did* defeat the First Wave — but the Second Wave was waiting up there, in space," explained the mystery Kroakan. "A hundred traceships — the fastest, deadliest vessels in the Kroakan armada — waiting to be awakened from farsleep, waiting for the summons of their prince ... you, Frog."

"I didn't summons anyone! I would've remembered," protested Frog.

"No, but *someone* did," replied the mystery Kroakan. "You remember that black orb I destroyed back in the forest? It was a probe, sent to find you and transmit the status of the Kroakan invasion back to King Kroak. Whoever activated that probe has doomed this world for a second time. But who—?"

"But you shot that orb to ka-bits with your arrow," said Frog, hobbling to keep up.

"Too late to stop it from sending its message," replied the mystery Kroakan.

"King Kroak must have found out that the First Wave had failed and activated the Second Wave remotely. The traceships will decimate Kingdomland! Those who survive the attack will be enslaved to rebuild the Ended World in the image of Kroakas."

"Death or enslavement — so much to look forward to," huffed the rarewolf.

"*Wait a minstrel* — did you understand what she said?" asked Frog. "You're speaking English — I thought Kroakans only spoke outer space speak."

"I'm ... not like most Kroakans," replied the mystery Kroakan, the sound of the valley's destruction a muffled echo in the distance. "Now, keep moving..."

"Not 'til I get some answers," replied Frog, halting in his tracks. "You appear out of nowhere, speaking this world's speak and wearing this world's clothes and hanging out with the rarewolf? You're the biggest plop of mystery in my big bucket of questions! Who are you?"

The mystery Kroakan stopped and turned back to face Frog.

"You're right," she sighed. "I do owe you an explanation."

"Really?" growled the rarewolf. "You want to get things off your chest *now*? Amidst the explosions and the fire and the horror?"

The mystery Kroakan ignored him. She kneeled down in front of Frog and peered at him intently.

"Are you giving me the evil psychic space eye?" asked Frog, suspiciously.

"My name is Kryl," began the mystery Kroakan. "I was on the farship that brought you to this world as an egg — the same ship that you found at the bottom of the royal lake before you awakened the First Wave. In fact, I was the farship's pilot."

"So you *are* one of them – I mean, you're an actual outer space invader," said Frog. "Do we have to fight now?"

"Of course not!" the mystery Kroakan assured him. "I am not a warrior, Frog, and I have no interest in King Kroak's invasion. I am a Keeper – *your* Keeper. I made a solemn oath to protect and care for you, from egg to prince."

"Keeper?" said Frog, recalling his first, frantic meeting with General Kurg and his troops, not three days ago. "The general said my Keeper totally definitely died."

"I almost did," Kryl replied, shooting the rarewolf a withering look. "Our farship had entered this planet's atmosphere when it was

… struck by lightning."

"Well, excuse me for trying to prevent a thousand-year-old prophecy of doom!" huffed the rarewolf.

"Wait, *you* made the farship crash?" asked Frog.

"I thought it was for the best! What's the point of being a god of the storm if I can't use my lightning to shoot down alien invaders?" snarled the rarewolf.

"The point is, I managed to crash-land in a lake … the lake of the royal palace," continued Kryl. "But I was trapped in the wreckage as the farship flooded. By the time I freed myself, I found that you – or rather, your egg – had floated out of the ship and up to the surface. So I abandoned the farsleeping crew and went looking for you. But when I emerged from the lake, you were gone. I'd lost you."

"Princess Rainbow found my egg on the shore — she thought I was treasure and took me back to the palace," said Frog.

"You're missing the point!" growled the rarewolf. "This isn't about blasted eggs and princesses ... this is about destiny!"

"Leave him be," said Kryl. "He's been through enough."

"*He's* been through enough? *He's* the reason we're in this mess!" growled the rarewolf, rounding on Frog, his teeth bared. "Do you remember the ancient prophecy I spoke of when we first met, Frog? I never told you what the prophecy said, did I?"

"You ... said it was about the End of the World," Frog answered, quietly.

"Oh, but that's not all," sneered the rarewolf. "The prophecy spoke of a visitor from the stars — a visitor who is destined to bring about the End of the World. That visitor is *you*, Frog, I am sure of it."

"Me?" said Frog, his back pressed up against the cave wall. "Wait … if you knew I was supposed to end the world all this time, why didn't you just tell me? Why did you let me go to the palace and find the farship and wake up the invaders?"

"Because I interfered with destiny once and it cost me dear!" roared the rarewolf. He leaned forward, his breath hot on Frog's face. "And because there is a *second* part to the prophecy. It states that only the visitor destined to end the world … can save it."

"But that's bonkers," said Frog. "Who would end the world and then save it?"

"It's a prophecy! I don't make the rules! A prophecy just … is," snapped the rarewolf.

"But you chose your fate! You chose to rebel against the invaders. You chose to fight … so fight!"

"But I can't fight anything. Look at me!" said Frog. "I can't even defeat one queen. I'm not mighty and I'm not a prince. I can't save the world – my mightiness is a myth!"

"But the prophecy—" roared the rarewolf.

"Is bumdrops! Don't you get it? It's nothing! *I'm* nothing!" cried Frog. "Just … leave me alone!"

With that, Frog threw his sword to the ground and raced down the tunnel.

The Difference Between "Aaah" and "Baa"

"Frog! Wait!"

Kryl's voice echoed through the labyrinth of tunnels, but Frog did not stop. He wanted to escape. From the rarewolf … from the End of the World … from his destiny. Tears blurred his vision as the luminous blue light began to fade. He ran blindly through the gloom, until his foot caught on a sharp rock. He tripped and tumbled to the ground with a…

THRUD-CH.

Frog lay there on the cold, damp earth, choking back tears and hoping the darkness would swallow him, hoping he could disappear … but fate was not so kind.

After a few moments he heard footsteps approaching, too quick to be Kryl or the rarewolf. Frog had no mighty weapons — no mightiness at all — and no fight left in him. He closed his eyes...

"Baa."

Frog reopened one eye and peered into the gloom. A small, round shape stood in front of him.

"Sheriff ... Explosion?" whimpered Frog. He felt a wet nose nuzzle his face.

"Baa."

"Sheriff Explosion, it *is* you!" he said, hugging the sheep and getting a whiff of singed wool. "Are you all right? How did you find me?"

"Baa," replied Sheriff Explosion, doing no justice to the terrifying ordeal he'd suffered to get there.

"Everything's gone to plops, Sheriff," Frog said. "I'm not a champion … I'm not even mighty. Turns out the only thing I'm good at is making the world end, which is basically the worst thing to be good at. Look at me! Even my catastrophe pants are showing signs of catastrophe…"

Frog tugged at his shorts, charred and ragged from his encounters.

"Well, I'm done. You hear me, world? I'm finished! I've had enough! No more champion or prince or destiny. I'm going to sit here and not move and do nothing until I die. Sit here and die and be dead! Frog is dead! Long live Frog not being alive! Then they'll be sorry … except they probably won't 'cause no one cares about a stupid nothing nobody who isn't even a mighty anything! I wish I'd never left the island! Bumdrops to all of it!"

Sheriff Explosion stared at Frog blankly. "Baa."

Frog sighed and patted his sheep on the head. "I'm sorry, Sheriff," he said. "I understand if you don't want to be my trusty steed any more…"

The sheep stood silently in the darkness for a moment. Then it sat down next to Frog and pressed itself up against him.

"Baa," it said.

"Thanks," Frog sniffed. He sat up slowly and wiped the tears from his face. "I miss the island. I miss Buttercup."

"Baa."

"Aaah!"

"Wait, did you say, 'Baa' or 'Aaah'?" asked Frog.

"Baa?" replied Sheriff Explosion.

"I thought so," said Frog. "That's a relief, I thought I was going—"

"Aaah!"

"OK, that was definitely wasn't 'baa'... that was someone – someone in double trouble," Frog began. He was about leap to his feet, when he stopped and slumped back down. "Except ... this is champion business. This is just the sort of thing I just said I wasn't doing any more. Someone else should handle—"

"AAAAH!"

"Well, maybe just a quick look, since they're in *double* trouble," he sighed, dragging himself to his feet. "Come on, Sheriff Explosion..."

The Mouse-Louse

Frog ran and hopped as fast as the darkness and his considerable bruising would allow. After three trips and two good falls, he and Sheriff Explosion stumbled into a low, blue-lit chamber. It was filled with a modest collection of poorly made furniture, and occupied by:

Princess Rainbow

Man-Lor the barbarian

Nigel the bragon

A cow-sized woodlouse with a mouse's head and a long pink tail.

"What the ... what?" muttered Frog, as he watched the half-louse, half-mouse pin Man-Lor to the ground, its buck-toothed jaws gnashing inches from the barbarian's face. "Am I UnSlumbering again?"

"Greeny! Save us from the icky thing!" cried Princess Rainbow, throwing rocks at the creature's hard shell.

"This might be the loop-de-doopiest thing I've ever seen," shrugged Frog. "The whole world is being blown to pieces by alien space invaders and you're wasting your fight on that thing? What is it?"

"A mouse-louse!" replied the bragon, trying to drag the slavering creature off Man-Lor by its tail. "When the sky fell we fled to my old abode in the caves – only to find a mouse-louse here, drinking my tea. And he's been using the good cups!"

"Man-Lor has drool in hair," groaned Man-Lor, as he struggled against the mouse-louse. "Please help Man-Lor."

"Do something, Greeny!" squealed the princess. "We're going to be eaten!"

"I'm sorry, are you talking to me? The mighty champion who just got beaten up by your *mum*?" replied Frog. "For the last time, I can't do anything. I'm not a champion. I don't even have any mighty weapons!"

He tugged at his catastrophe pants and felt something in his pocket. He reached in and retrieved the magical talisman he'd taken from the blue house in the sky.

"See? All I've got is a whizz-bang wizard whatsit," he huffed. "Load of old bumdrops…"

Frog tossed the talisman in frustration. It landed on the mouse-louse's shell and exploded in a flash.

"SKREE-EE!"

The mouse-louse shrieked in fright as shimmering golden light engulfed it. A moment later, the beast began to shrink before Frog's eyes. By the time the glow subsided, the mouse-louse was no bigger than … a mouse. Frog watched it scuttle fearfully into the darkness.

"Baa," noted an impressed Sheriff Explosion.

"Greeny saved Man-Lor," said Man-Lor, scrabbling to his feet. "I am Man-Lor."

"Pfff – still doesn't make me a champion," huffed Frog.

"Well something must," said a voice.

Frog turned to see the rarewolf clamber into the cave, with Kryl following close behind. "Because if you can't save us, the whole of Kingdomland is doomed."

The Return to the Palace

"Save the world yourself," sighed Frog, as the rarewolf paced around him. "Just leave me alone."

"I can't leave you alone," said Kryl, with a smile. "I'm your Keeper, remember. I promised to keep you safe."

Princess Rainbow pointed an outstretched arm at Kryl.

"You're one of the ay'lun space invaders," she said. "I like that you speak proper English and not gibby gobby goo. Mummy says everyone should speak proper—"

"Your mother? Ha!" growled the rarewolf. "If that witch even still lives, she'll be a slave to the—"

"Look!" interrupted Kryl, loudly. "The

155

whole invasion thing isn't ideal for anyone. But can we at least all agree that we want to make it out of here alive?"

"I command that, actually," said Princess Rainbow, glowering at the rarewolf.

"Good," continued Kryl. "We don't have long. The Kroakans will soon work out we've escaped to these caves and come looking for us. We need a way out of here."

"Man-Lor not go outside," said Man-Lor.

"Too right, by gosh," concurred the bragon, wiping mouse-louse slobber from his spectacles. "But these tunnels stretch for miles in every direction. All the way to the Upside-Downtains in the west and the royal palace in the east."

"Palace! Palace!" cried the princess, excitedly. "I can show you my pets!"

"We'll find no protection there,"

growled the rarewolf. "The palace was half-demolished by the last invasion."

"But I have to change my dress – this one has ay'lun space invader explosions all over it," said the princess matter-of-factly.

"Oh, well why didn't you say so?" snapped the rarewolf. "Let's all risk our lives for the sake of a dress!"

"No … the princess is right," interrupted Kryl, clenching her fist. "We should go to the palace. If it's already been decimated, perhaps the Kroakans won't think to look there…"

"That's the most ridiculous thing I ever—" the rarewolf began.

"Outvoted!" interrupted the princess, sticking out her tongue at the rarewolf. "Which way to the palace of Kin'domland, Nigel the bragon?"

The journey to the palace was long and cold, through dark tunnels and even darker passageways. After initial introductions, the odd assemblage remained largely quiet as they made their way through the gloom. Only the princess broke the silence, whiling away the hours by describing all three hundred and three of her dresses in detail. But after a while, even she grew tired and fell asleep in Man-Lor's arms.

Frog remained silent, as if his spirit had left him.

It was almost dawn by the time the travellers emerged, hungry and frozen, from the tunnels. They clambered out into the bitter air at the foot of a mountain. Frog recognized the place immediately. He had been here only three days ago, expecting to be welcomed with open arms as a prince of Kingdomland. He stared up at the ruins of the royal palace. Even though only two of its many towers and spires remained, it was still a sight to behold.

"Home?" yawned the princess, waking up. She looked up at the palace and rubbed her eyes. "So, first I'll eat polished sandwiches until I burp, which when you're a princess is called a 'royal hiccup'. And then I will show you all my crowns. And then we're going to play dressing up. And then— What's that smell?"

Frog sniffed the air. It smelled like a log fire. He slowly turned and peered out over Kingdomland.

"Yoiks…" he whispered.

Countless glowing red pools lit up the gloom. As far as the eye could see, fires raged.

"They're – they're all over Kingdomland," said the rarewolf, his eyes wide. "None of the six-and-a-half realms have been spared. Not even the half-realm…"

"Buttercup," began Frog. "I have to find her…"

"Your friend is all right, Frog, I promise – the island is shielded by a powerful spell,"said Kryl. She nudged the rarewolf in the ribs. "Isn't that right?"

"What? Oh yes, Buttercup is alive and well," the rarewolf grunted. "It's the rest of the world we need to worry about…"

"Mummy and Daddy will sort it all out," Princess Rainbow assured them. "They've fought the whole of Kin'domland and not lost a fight ever. Now, who wants to see my crowns?"

The Clothes Make the Frog

"Open the gates!" squealed the princess, as they made their way across a nerve-shredding, rickety, wooden bridge to the palace (the original bridge having been destroyed in the first invasion). "We're all going to dress up and have a tea party until the horrid things stop."

"Tea party?" repeated the bragon delightedly. "I'm gasping, by gosh!"

While the palace guards were relieved to find their princess safe, they were less happy about letting in her strange acquaintances, especially since Kroakans, rarewolves and bragons were all officially enemies of Kingdomland. But upon the princess's command, the remaining palace staff came out of hiding and prepared a breakfast of polished sandwiches, polished cakes and hot, polished tea.

In the relative safety of the palace's underground wine cellars, everyone ate their fill – but dread still gnawed away in the pit of Frog's stomach. How long before the traceships made their way to the palace? How long before all of Kingdomland was conquered?

"Dress-up time!" said Princess Rainbow, getting down from the table. "I'm going to wear my snow dress. Because it's – *buurp!* – snowing."

"Actually, we could all do with some warm, fresh clothes," suggested Kryl. "Perhaps a little 'dressing up' wouldn't be a bad idea. What do you think, Frog?"

Frog peered at his shredded cape and

threadbare catastrophe pants and pushed out a sigh.

"Fine … but nothing champion-style."

Twenty minutes later, the princess and her guests were dressed in fresh, warm clothes, collected from staff, sentries and even what remained of the King and Queen's wardrobe.

"I am *not* wearing this," Frog groaned, staring at himself in one of the princess's most flattering mirrors. His catastrophe pants were in a heap on the floor — instead the princess had dressed him in large, furry shorts, leather armour with an ornate golden clasp in the middle of his chest, and a particularly impressive furred cape. "I look all championed-up like a mighty barbarian … I look like Man-Lor!"

"I am Man-Lor," said Man-Lor.

"I think we all look first-rate, truth be told," noted Nigel, swishing his new scarlet scarf. "Almost makes me wish I wore more clothes."

"And it's better than looking like a homeless hob-gobbin," tutted Princess Rainbow, admiring her own bright, white dress, snow-crow feather-lined cape and icy silver tiara. "Where's your ay'lun friend? I've got a cape that will bring out the yellow of her ay'lun eyes…"

Frog looked around, but Kryl was no longer in the room. He turned to the rarewolf.

"She said she had something to take care of," he said with a shrug. "In the dungeon."

"The dungeon? What's in the— Waaait, unless…" said Frog. He raced out of the room as fast as his furry boots would carry him. "Come on, Sheriff Explosion!"

As Frog raced out of the changing chamber, Sheriff Explosion appeared sheepishly from behind a mirror, wearing thick, rosy lipstick and four of the princess's most sparkly shoes.

"Baa?"

The Last Resort

Frog hurried and hopped through the palace, looking for Kryl. Palace staff recoiled in horror as the green-skinned, furry-shorted creature ran past them.

"The dungeon!" he cried. "Where's the dungeon?"

Frog followed their nervous pointing, down a long stairwell into the servants' quarters. Then down again, into the underground chambers beneath the palace. He came to a long, white-walled corridor with a thick door at its end. He sped down it to find the door ajar.

"Kryl!" he cried. She was standing in the middle of the room, her bow drawn, an arrow ready to fire. In the centre of the cage, his feet shackled to the ground by thick chains, was General Kurg. The defeated Kroakan commander was even taller than Man-Lor, with dark-green skin and two large, orange-yellow eyes. Even stripped of his Kroakan battle armour, he was an imposing sight.

"By the Void! Prince Frog, you still live!" cried General Kurg. "How did you survive the Second Wave?"

"What are you doing, Kryl?" asked Frog. "You can't... Don't shoot him!"

"It was him, Frog. It was Kurg who activated the probe!" she hissed, her hand shaking as she kept the bowstring taut. "He's the reason they sent the traceships!"

"What? How's that even possible? He's been stuck in this dungeon the whole time," said Frog.

The general burst out laughing. "By the Smell of Victory! You have a lot to learn, O Prince. King Kroak leaves nothing to chance," scoffed General Kurg. He reached into his mouth and wrenched out a tooth.

"Yoiks..." blurted Frog. "And eww."

"This – ow – is my Mayday Molar,"

explained General Kurg, holding up the tooth. "The last resort of a Kroakan general. You see, only a king or prince may summon the Second Wave, but a general can use *this* to remotely activate a probe should the First Wave fail."

"You sent the orb to find me?" said Frog.

"The probe is programmed to search out all Kroakan life on the planet and beam its findings back to King Kroak," the general responded. "I can only assume by all the glorious explosions outside that your betrayal was discovered! It seems King Kroak has taken matters into his own hands…"

"Monster! You've doomed your own prince!" cried Kryl.

"By the Boot of Oppression! What did you expect me to do, admit defeat? I am a general in the Army of a Thousand Sons!

Space invading is my life!" growled Kurg. "And speaking of monsters, wait 'til you meet *Major Krass*. Now there's a Kroakan who scares even me…"

"You're going to pay for what you've done," snarled Kryl. "I'll *make* you pay."

Frog heard Kryl's bowstring stretch to its limit as she prepared to loose her arrow.

"Stop!" Frog cried. "What are you doing?"

"He cost us everything, Frog!" hissed Kryl, her eyes flooding red with rage. "He cost *me* everything!"

"Look, I wish I could flush General Kurg down a bottomless toilet made of spikes and fire – of course I do," began Frog. "But Buttercup told me that I was meant to be good – that I must always make the right choice. This isn't that. This is bad."

Kryl held her breath for a long, silent

moment. Then she lowered her bow, fell to her knees and began to sob. Frog walked over to her and put his hand on her shoulder.

"I'm sorry, Frog," Kryl wept. "I'm so sorry."

"Don't be sorry, everything's going to be all right," Frog replied. "I mean, I think everything's hopefully maybe going to be all right."

"By the Imperial Underwear! What mawkish slush," groaned General Kurg. "Major Krass is going to tear you to pieces, Frog."

"Shut up! You're still in big fat troubles, General," snapped Frog. "I'm going to leave you down here forever … and make sure they only feed you burpy turnips."

"Frog!" came a cry. Frog turned to see the bragon appear at the door, the rarewolf and

Sheriff Explosion following behind.

"It's Princess Rainbow," continued the bragon. "She said she wanted to see 'Mummy and Daddy defeat the invaders'. She said she was going back to the blue house."

"What? But it's miles to the blue— Wait, the secret door. She's going back there!" Frog leaped to his feet and turned to his trusty steed. "Come on, Sher— Wait, are you wearing *lipstick*?"

"Baa," replied the sheep.

"Bonkers," he sighed.

The Last of the Rarewolves

Frog and the others hurried back up the palace stairs. With the rarewolf following the princess's plum-petal scent, they raced up and up into the once-regal, now-blasted parts of the palace. Finally, they emerged in a half-disintegrated chamber marked *Royal Wizard's Room — Please Knock (Princesses Exempt From Knocking)* — and stepped inside.

What remained of the room was empty except for a blue door, slightly ajar. Frog made his way over to it. Written on the door in neat letters were the words:

KEEP OUT.
NO SECRET MAGIC WIZARD THINGS WITHIN.
AT ALL. NOT ONE.

175

And underneath that, in smaller letters:

IF YOU'RE STILL READING YOU'VE PROBABLY
REALIZED THERE CERTAINLY ARE SECRET MAGIC
WIZARD THINGS WITHIN.
PLEASE KEEP OUT ALL THE SAME.

Frog tutted and pushed open the door. There was the front room of the blue house, just as they had left it the previous day. He stepped inside and saw Princess Rainbow at the far end of the room, staring out of the window, down into the valley.

"Frog," said the princess, softly. "What has happened to my mummy and daddy?"

Frog walked slowly over to the window … and looked down.

Dawn light shone over the horizon, illuminating the devastation. Where once stood proud, crimson mountains were piles of smouldering rubble. Ten or more traceships had landed on the ground and deposited their sinister occupants. Frog saw dozens upon dozens of Kroakan troopers, each clad in black armour and armed with sunder-guns.

And in the centre of what remained of the valley, covered by a glowing dome of green energy, was a huddled crowd of survivors, fifty at most ... all that was left of the royal army.

"Yoiks..." Frog muttered, peering closer through the gathering clouds. Was the Queen down there? The King? Captain Camperlash?

"How's my valley?" said the bragon, squeezing nervously through the blue door and into the house, closely followed by Kryl, Man-Lor and Sheriff Explosion. "How does it look?"

"Bad," replied Frog. "It's all the badness there is, plus a million."

Everyone had been staring out of the window for more than a minute — except for the rarewolf, who had managed to get himself stuck halfway through the door. His front end now resided in the Omnium Gatherum, while his backside remained firmly in the palace.

"Why haven't they ka-boomed the blue house?" Frog asked, finally breaking the silence.

"This house is magic," replied Kryl. "They probably don't even know we're here."

"You have to save my mummy and daddy, Greeny," said Princess Rainbow, tugging Frog's furry shorts. "They're down there, I know they are. You can save them."

"Princess—" began Frog.

"Don't you dare, Frog!" shouted the rarewolf, struggling to break free of the doorway. "I want you to save the world more than anyone, but there's no point in risking your life to save the King and Queen ... even if they are still alive."

"Yes, they're alive! They're very alive! Don't say those things, you *emeny* of Kin'domland!" squealed the princess. She turned back to Frog, tears in her eyes. "Please, Frog... Please save my mummy and daddy."

"But ... that's champion business," Frog began. "I told you, I'm not—"

"Frog!" the rarewolf growled. "I never told you how I came to be the last of the rarewolves, did I?"

"What's that got to do with—?" Frog began.

"Just listen," the rarewolf growled. "You remember how I used the lightning to bring down your farship? Well, I went to check there were no survivors ... and discovered the ship had crashed in the grounds of the palace. I tried to warn the Queen of the danger, but she would not let me in. With the prophecy weighing heavy on my mind, I broke into the palace."

"Bad rarewolf," tutted Princess Rainbow.

"I followed the Kroakan scent – the scent of your egg – to the princess's chambers," the rarewolf continued. "But no sooner had I got there than I was overwhelmed by the Queen and her guards. I had spent all my lightning crashing the alien ship ... I was as weak as a cub. So I fled. That was the day the Queen declared war on all rarewolves! Because they thought I meant to harm their daughter, they hunted us down – rooted out my brothers and sisters and murdered them. They called it a war against the enemies of peace ... but it was a slaughter."

"The Queen killed the rarewolves?" asked Frog.

"Every one ... except me. I ran away and I haven't stopped running since," replied the rarewolf. "So, believe me, the King and Queen of Everything are not worth saving!"

"Shut up!" said Princess Rainbow. "I'm the princess, so shut up!"

"The Queen defeated you, Frog!" continued the rarewolf. "She thrashed you and humiliated you in front of everyone! Why risk your life for her?"

Frog stared out of the window, up into the morning sky. Finally he said, "Because it's the right choice."

He turned slowly.

"Prophecies and destinies are a load of plops," he continued. "But that doesn't change the fact there's a load of folks down there who needs saving, maybe a whole world of folks, and even if the folks who need saving wouldn't save me if I needed saving – even if they'd rather chop my head off – I still can't not save those folks without being bad for not saving them. And not being mighty isn't a reason to not save the folks who are in need of saving … even if that means I get killed to bits."

"Is anyone else confused?" asked the bragon.

"Frog, please, you don't have to—" began Kryl.

"What I mean is, I might not be mighty," continued Frog. "But I'm all dressed up like a champion, so it's time to do some champion business."

"Do it, by gosh!" cried the bragon.

"Together," Frog said.

"Oh, poo," said the bragon.

The Excellent Magicals and the Champion Business

Frog quickly concocted a plan to rescue the prisoners of the Kroakan army. It was worryingly vague, but with every reference to "excellent magicals" and "champion business" he seemed to regain a measure of his old confidence. One thing had changed, however. Frog knew he could be defeated ... he knew he could lose.

"So, is everyone ready?" he asked, piling up talisman-filled boxes next to the front door.

The motley assortment of creatures in the Omnium Gatherum stared back at him in silence. It comprised:

- Princess Rainbow! Daughter of the King and Queen of Everything, heir to the throne of Kingdomland, wearer of sparkly dresses.

- Kryl! Kroakan Keeper, reluctant space invader.
- Nigel the bragon! Many-named boast-beast, lover of flying and tea.
- The Rarewolf! Ancient, snow-allergic storm god, last of his kind, currently stuck halfway between the royal palace and the Omnium Gatherum.
- Man-Lor! Barbarian, furry-panted protector of Princess Rainbow, secret poetry writer.
- Sheriff Explosion! Sheep in high heels.

"May I be the first to say, this plan sounds altogether fatal," said the bragon.

"I agree," added Kryl. "It's too dangerous. Even if it works — which it can't possibly — you'll be putting yourself in mortal danger."

"Worst plan ever!" echoed the rarewolf from the doorway.

"I like your stupid plan, Greeny," said Princess Rainbow. "I b'lieve in it."

"That's 'cause it's a bold and thrill-venturous plan! Whether it works or not," concluded Frog. He took off his cape and collected the corners into a sack shape. Then he scooped a large handful of talismans from one of the boxes and filled the cape. "Timing is everything – and excellent magicals," he added, taking a last talisman out of the box and popping it into his pocket. "And we're going to need a lot of flying time, Nigel – you'll have to fill up."

"Fine…" sighed the bragon. "But I'm only doing this because you sort of slightly saved my life, by gosh." He took off his spectacles and placed them on the blue table. Then he ran his claws through his plume of purple hair. "The Duke lives to fly, by gosh … for the Duke rules the sky!" His voice was suddenly booming and resonant.

He opened the front door and stepped out on to the porch as he began to swell. "The Duke's legend is known from the Lesser Lakes to the Higher Plains! The Duke could outfly a hundred sunbirds with his wings in chains! The Duke could zoom to the moon without catching cold! The Duke could soar into the sun and come back with a tan! You stand before the Quotable Gloatable, Sir Bestalot, the Baron of Bravadonia, Unimpeachable Maximus, Grandiloquence Gasconade … Duke Bombastion the Many-Named!"

"Baa!" bleated Sheriff Explosion

encouragingly, as the bragon expanded at an alarming rate.

"The Duke is twice as strong as you, barbarian!" he said, pointing at Man-Lor. "The Duke is ten times more fearsome than you, rarewolf! The Duke's bogies are a hundred times greener than you, Kryl! The Duke is a thousand times more sparkly than you, Princess!"

"I don't like the bragon any more," the princess grumbled, folding her arms huffily.

"The Duke is a million times mightier than you, Frog!" the bragon continued, filling like a balloon.

"Keep going!" insisted Frog.

"A *billion* times mightier! A jillion! Is a jillion a number?" cried the bragon, swollen to bursting point. "Can't ... boast ... any more!"

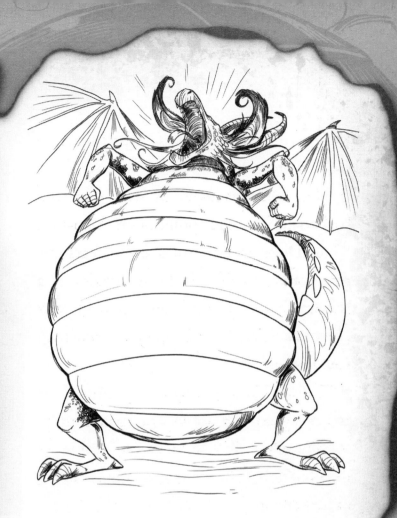

"That'll do!" cried Frog. Frog twisted the top of his cape full of talismans and flung it over his shoulder. Then he raced out of the front door and leaped on to the bragon's back. "Everyone remember the plan!"

"Frog, wait!" cried Kryl. She rushed over to him, and produced Frog's magical sword from inside her robe.

"You ... dropped it in the caves," she said. "I thought you might need it."

"Thanks – I think I might," Frog replied, taking the sword and sliding it into its scabbard. A moment later the bragon leapt out of the doorway.

The Battle in the Sky

"WAaaA-HOOO!" cried Frog, hanging on to the bragon's scarf as they soared majestically through the air.

"You will at least try not to get us killed, won't you?" pleaded the bragon.

"Just take us as low as you can!" Frog replied. "But don't spend all your air!"

BUU-U-RRRRRP!

With a thunderous belch, the bragon let out half his air and immediately began nose-diving towards the ground. The clouds were gathering fast, and it took them a moment to get a close look at the Kroakan camp. Frog counted ten traceships on the ground.

"Lower!" cried Frog.

"If we get any lower, they'll spot us!"

insisted the bragon.

"Weren't you listening to the plan?" said Frog. "That's the idea!"

"Were you not listening when I said I was a coward?" The bragon sighed. "Just hang on tight…"

BUURRRRRP!

The bragon plunged downwards, swooping over the Kroakan camp. Frog looked down and saw the oil-black hulls of the traceships below them. He held out his cape full of magical talismans. "Closer!"

"This feels pretty close, truth be told!" shrieked the bragon.

"Just hold it steady!" cried Frog. He took a deep breath and opened his cape, scattering the talismans over the tops of the traceships.

The enchanted stones exploded upon impact, creating a plethora of magical effects – a fireball, a flash of light, a shower of spiralling fireworks. One talisman sprouted into a mighty tree in the blink of an eye, whose branches engulfed one of the traceships, swallowing it as the trunk reached skywards. Another traceship was turned completely inside out, expelling its pilot like a gob of spit. A third stone caused living skeletons to appear from out of the ground and flay the invaders with bony fingers, and a fourth created a tidal wave, which swept a dozen Kroakans down the valley.

"Yoiks... *Excellent* magicals," whispered Frog in awe. He looked back to see the Kroakans in turmoil. Some tried to find cover, while others opened fire on their own ships.

"We're under attack!"

"Reality is unfolding!"

"Shoot everything! It's the only way to be sure!"

"That got their attention, Nigel," cried Frog. "Now get us out of the valley!"

"*That* part of the plan I like, by gosh," muttered the bragon – but the Kroakan troopers turned their attention upon this strange, unknown flying object.

As the bragon sank ever closer to the ground, sunder-beams streaked past his head, setting fire to his hair plume. Frog frantically patted out the flames as the bragon shrieked in terror. But after a few more wing beats, the sunder-beams started to miss their mark entirely – they were out of range. Frog looked back again. From inside one of the traceships, he saw a huge figure emerge – bigger than any Kroakan he'd ever seen.

"Yoiks…" Frog muttered. "Who is that?"

Frog saw the giant Kroakan draw a sunder-gun and take aim.

"No way," said Frog. "We're too far away. We've got to be too—"

Frog saw a flash of green energy – and felt a searing pain shoot through his right arm. He cried out, barely managing to hang on.

"Frog!" cried the bragon, as Frog held on for dear life.

"I'm fine! Go!" cried Frog, glancing at the smoking burn on his arm. He dared to look back one more time, and saw the Kroakans man the remaining traceships. In seconds, all ten of them had taken to the air.

"They're following us, Nigel – the plan's working!" said Frog. "Now climb!"

"I'm out of air!" the bragon replied. "I'll never get high enough!"

"Boast, Nigel!" cried Frog. "Boast … boast like the wind!"

"I … I … I…!" began the bragon, in a blind panic. "I can't think! My mind's gone blank!"

Frog heard the low, grating hum of the traceships grow louder as they gave chase.

"You can do it, Nigel! You're mightier by

a million! Say it!"

"I-I'm mightier by a million...?" muttered the bragon, unconvinced.

"Keep going!" said Frog. "You've just baked the quiche of defeat and everyone's getting a slice!"

"I-I've just baked the quiche of defeat ... and everyone's getting a slice!" repeated the bragon – and started swelling.

"You're going to move into a house of victory and use them as a welcome mat!" said Frog.

"I am! I'm going to move into a house of victory and use them as a welcome mat!" yelled the bragon, the hot air filling him.

"You're the mightiest champion of—!" Frog began.

"The Duke is the mightiest champion of Kingdomland ever!" hollered the bragon, swollen to balloon-like proportions.

"It's working!" Frog cried. As they rocketed towards the cloudline, Frog peered upwards. The hum of the traceships was still growing louder — they were seconds away. "The cloud's too thick — can't see the house ... Come on, Kryl, where are you?"

Rays of green lit up the sky, as the traceships opened fire. The bragon howled, banking and spinning wildly to avoid the rays. One of the traceships broke formation, zooming ahead. It raced towards them, sunder-beams blazing ... it would be on them in seconds.

"We're not going to make it," Frog whispered to himself. He winced in pain as he wrapped the bragon's scarf around his wounded arm. Then he drew his magical sword. "Nigel! Tuck in your wings!"

"But—" began the bragon.

"Do it! Do it now!"

As a sunder-beam seared his tail, the bragon pulled his wings into his body, slowing enough that the traceship raced over the top of them, almost close enough to touch.

Do your thing, Basil Rathbone! Frog thought, thrusting the blade into the traceship as it passed overhead. The invincible blade sliced along the length of ship, cutting through the thick metal like it was butter, sending fire and sparks exploding from within. The traceship veered away and spun helplessly to the ground.

"OK … that was pretty mighty," Frog admitted with a grin.

"One down, loads to go!" howled the bragon, frantically searching the skies as the remaining traceships gained fast. "Where's the house, by——?"

Suddenly, the Omnium Gatherum burst through the clouds, soaring through the air towards them, banking and weaving as if it was drunk.

"There they are!" cried Princess Rainbow from inside the blue house. She pointed out of the window as the bragon appeared in their sights. "Down there, that way!"

"I'm trying! I've never piloted a *house* before…" replied Kryl, wrestling with the wooden handle as she navigated the Omnium Gatherum through the sky. "Open the doors and get ready… Wait 'til the bragon passes!"

Outside, the bragon put himself on a collision course with the house. He could see the princess and Man-Lor waiting at the open door.

"Get underneath it, Nigel! We have to time this just right..." yelled Frog. With the smallest of burps, the bragon pumped his wings and swooped underneath the house. Frog saw blue stone rush over his head. He glanced in the gleaming blade of his magical sword and saw the reflection of the traceships...

"Now!"

He and Kryl and the princess cried out at the same moment.

Man-Lor added, "I am Man-Lor!" at the top of his lungs — and pushed the stack of blue boxes out of the door. In that moment, the traceships passed underneath the house, sunder-beams blazing, the boxes exploded on their metal hulls, detonating every one of the hundreds of talismans within.

The effect was magical.

The myriad explosions of light, sparks, fireworks and flame was enough to temporarily blind the traceship's pilots. One immediately veered off into another, sending them both spiralling out of control ... by which time the effects of the spell-binding talismans had taken effect on the other traceships.

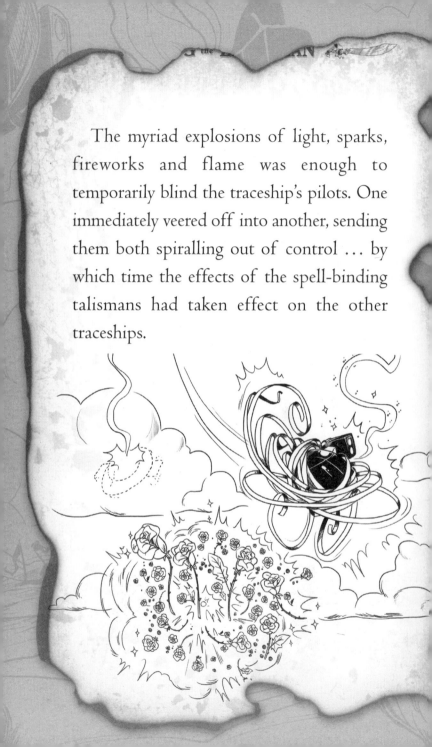

"Yoiks…" muttered Frog. He saw one traceship unravel like it was made from strips of silk; the second exploded into a million bright, white roses; the third was stretched so thinly it disappeared; the fourth turned to ice; the fifth to wood; the sixth to lemon jelly … and the seventh became a colossal, burpy turnip.

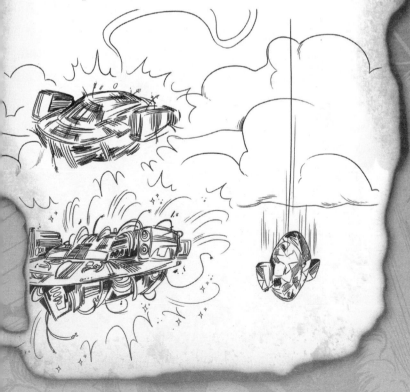

In the end, not a single traceship remained in the air.

"They did it ... they did it!" Frog cried. The bragon flew alongside the house as Princess Rainbow stuck her head out of the window.

"Look, Greeny!" she shouted, pointing to the transformed and transmogrified traceships that plummeted to their doom. "You're stupid plan wasn't even that stupid!"

"What did I tell you? Excellent magicals!" he grinned, giving her a thumbs-up. "Now let's get down there and do some saving."

The Major

By now, the Kroakan troops on the ground were panicking. They had just seen their entire fleet of traceships meet strange and unbelievable fates in the skies above them. They found cover behind rocks and took aim with their sunder-guns. Only one of the troopers remained out in the open – the giant Kroakan who had shot Frog stood directly in front of the prisoner-filled energy dome.

"Major Krass!" cried one of the troopers. "Our traceships are gone! What are your orders?"

"Shut up, for starters," replied Major Krass in a deep, gravel-crunching growl. He was unfeasibly wide and bulky – and almost twice as tall as General Kurg. His sleek, black armour seemed unable to contain him, as he drew an oversized pair of sunder-guns. "I'll handle this."

The major watched the bragon swoop down from the sky and land in front of him.

"Are you sure this is a good idea?" Nigel whispered to Frog, who still clung on to the bragon's scarf. "I've got no air to spare…"

"Trust me," replied Frog. "I need to do this."

He leaped down from the bragon, his wounded arm hanging limply by his side. The Kroakan troopers gasped to see their prince standing before them – two even kneeled down. But Major Krass did not flinch.

"I am Frog!" he cried. With his good arm he pointed at the dome. "Free the prisoners! I seriously mean it!"

"I am Major Krass of the Army of a Thousand Sons," thundered the major. "Spawn Five-One-Three, I presume. I heard you rebelled … I didn't realize you'd gone *native*. Are you wearing furry shorts?"

"They're actually super-warm on my rump-end," admitted Frog. "Now I mean it – release them, or *else*."

"Or else what?" asked the major, unimpressed.

"Yes, or else what?" whispered the bragon, nervously.

"Or else, that," Frog answered, and looked up. The blue house floated down from the sky above them, casting a shadow over the troops as it hovered in the air. "There's enough excellent magicals up there to mess up your whole business – just like we messed up your traceships! Now release the prisoners!"

"The sunder-dome remains closed," replied Major Krass, matter-of-factly. He pressed a button on his sunder-guns and shimmering blades of green energy appeared from their barrels. "If you want the prisoners, you'll have to take them. From me."

"Frog, don't!" came a cry. Frog looked up to see Kryl's head poking out of the window. "You have nothing to prove!"

Frog let a long, heavy sigh leave his body. "Yes, I do," he said. He straightened himself up, took a deep breath of cold morning air and slowly drew his sword with a quivering hand. Then he fixed his gaze upon Major Krass. "I'm warning you — these furry shorts aren't just for show. I'm a full-on barbarian."

The Major's bulbous yellow eye twitched.

"Then fight me ... 'barbarian'," he replied.

Frog gripped his sword tightly. "I'm going to get *medieval* on you, Krass."

The Barbarian

"RaaAAAArgh!" cried Frog, bounding towards the major, his sword drawn. Krass brought his sunder-swords to bear. In a single, fluid movement he parried Frog's sword stroke and spun around with a kick, sending Frog flying into the scorched earth.

"Frog!" cried Kryl and Princess Rainbow.

"RaaAAargh!" Frog cried again, leaping to his feet, his eyes flooding red. He threw himself at Krass, but this time the major deflected Basil Rathbone with both sunder-swords and brought an elbow up into Frog's face.

As Frog felt one of his teeth shoot to the back of his mouth, Krass kicked out with a giant knee. Frog flew through the air again and skidded along the rubble-strewn ground.

"King Kroak doesn't care whether I bring you in dead or alive, Spawn Five-One-Three," said Krass. "But you'll take up less space in my ship if you're dead."

Frog struggled to his feet. He leaped at the major a third time. With one sunder-sword, the major sent Basil Rathbone flying out of Frog's hand and though the air. Then he brought the other blade down across Frog's face.

Frog cried out, tumbling to the ground, a burning cut across his left eye.

"Urgh!" grunted Frog, more from pain than rage. Once again, he dragged himself to his feet – but this time Major Krass simply stomped him back into the rubble. Frog tried to get up... And again he found himself pushed face first into the ruins of the valley.

"This world will burn, rebel," said Major Krass, grinding Frog with his foot. "The traceships are already scorching every corner of this pathetic planet. I don't know what you see in it, I really don't…"

Frog squealed as the Major rolled him on to his back with his foot.

"So, trust me when I tell you, Spawn Five-One-Three, I am going to destroy everything you ever cared about," the major continued. "I will set this world alight, and bring unbridled misery to its people. And I'll do it all before breakfast."

The major squeezed the last breath out of Frog's lungs with a huge foot.

"And even after you are dust, I will make it my mission to bring suffering to everyone that ever mattered to you on this world. I will tarnish your memory and ruin every good thing you ever tried to do. Because I love my job. Because I *can*."

"Excellent ... magicals..." Frog wheezed.

"What?" barked Major Krass, lifting his boot off Frog's chest. "Speak up, traitor."

"I said ... excellent magicals," Frog gasped again.

"What of them?" grunted the major. Frog smiled.

"I kept one," he replied. Frog opened his right hand. He was holding a talisman with two circles carved into it – one large, one small. With the last of his strength he threw it at the major's chest. It exploded upon impact and Major Krass was engulfed in a shimmering golden light.

A moment later, he was no bigger than a mouse.

"What is this? Undo this madness! I command it!" the major squeaked in a tiny voice.

Frog sat up slowly and plucked him off the ground, holding him between two fingers. Then he looked up at the house, to see the princess, Kryl and Man-Lor poised with yet more magic-filled boxes.

Frog nodded. "Let 'em have it," he said.

The Prisoners

As it turned out, the sight of their leader shrunk down to mouse size — and having nine boxes of magic talismans dumped on their heads — was more than enough to send the remaining Kroakan troopers fleeing into the caves.

"Frog! You did it!" cried Kryl, as she brought the house to a bumpy landing in the middle of the ruined valley. "Are you all right?"

Frog stood up and dusted himself off, staring at the tiny, rage-filled Kroakan Major in his hands.

"I'm… I'm…" Frog began, the dislodged tooth falling out of his mouth. "I'm mightier than ever! Did you see my skilled-up moves with the talisman? KA-SHRINK! And look! I've got a new pet mini-Kroakan and everything."

"You will die in agony! You will rue the day! You will— Nooooooo...!" squeaked Major Krass, as Frog slipped him into the pocket of his furry shorts.

"Glad to see you're back to your old self," said Kryl with a smile.

"Greeny!" the princess cried. Frog turned to see her pointing at the sunder-dome. "Make this thing go away, Greeny!"

"I was just getting to that, actually," replied Frog, picking up Basil Rathbone. With a few slashes from his magical sword, the dome of energy vanished into nothing. Forty or so prisoners spilled out, wounded, dazed and relieved, into the valley.

"Mummy? Daddy?" squeaked Princess

Rainbow, pushing through the crowd of soldiers. "Where are you?"

Frog held his breath, scouring the crowd through swollen eyes. Then, finally:

"Give the Majesties some air, y' slopes!" came a cry. The crowd parted, and Captain Camperlash stepped out, carrying the King of Everything in his arms.

"Daddy!" Princess Rainbow cried, racing over to them. As Camperlash laid the King carefully on the ground, the princess ran into her father's arms.

"Oh, my little peapod! How I missed you!" wept the King happily. "Did you see the End of the World? What a show! I can't wait to see it again!"

"I *said* you were alive! And I said that Greeny should save you, so he did!" she said, tears in her eyes. "But where is—?"

"I'm here, Rainbow," replied the Queen, limping out of the crowd of soldiers. "Come and give your mother a hug."

"She's alive? Curses!" cried the rarewolf from inside the house.

"What are you doing consorting with these enemies of Kingdomland, Rainbow?" asked the Queen, glowering at Frog as the princess hugged her. "And what have I told you about having friends?"

"I know, Mummy," the princess replied. "But everything went wrong and blowed up and I didn't know what to do and you weren't there."

"Don't worry, I'm here now – I'll sort out everything," said the Queen. She pointed at Frog. "Captain Camperlash, *seize* this traitorous creature. And seize his companions while you're at it!"

"What the bumbles?" Frog blurted.

"Y' Majesty?" blurted Camperlash.

"Mummy!" snapped the princess.

"Can't you see? He's one of them... An invader! An enemy of Kingdomland!" the Queen hissed.

"Oh, this is bonkers," whispered Frog. He held up his sword again, as he, Kryl, the bragon and Sheriff Explosion gathered together, ready for yet another fight...

"Mummy, stop it!" protested Princess Rainbow. "Frog saved you!"

"Greeny save us all," added Man-Lor. "I am Man-Lor."

"Look around! The World is Ending! We must restore peace! We must destroy our enemies! We must—" began the Queen.

"Can't we just have peas and quiet for once?" interrupted the King, staring up into the sky. "I'm not even sure what day it is, but I know starting another fight now is *madness*. I mean, it's not as if it's the End of the World..."

"But ... but ... *fine*," the Queen grumbled. Then she looked at Princess Rainbow, and smiled. "It's good to see you again, little poppet."

Frog watched the King, Queen and Princess of Everything embrace. Man-Lor and Camperlash stood close by, both trying to remember the last time anyone had hugged them.

"Looks like the family's back together," Frog smiled. He glanced down and saw Sheriff Explosion nuzzle his leg.

"Baa."

"You said it," said Frog. "Let's get out of here."

The Second Part of the Prophecy

Frog didn't wait around to say goodbye to the princess – he and his trusty steed made their way back inside the blue house. Kryl and the bragon were already inside, struggling to free the rarewolf as he grumbled about his predicament.

"You should have – ow! – seen all my champion business, rarewolf! I was so mighty that I could have defeated a million traceships ... maybe even a hundred!" cried Frog, as he limped inside, prodding the impressive scar over his left eye. "You were right – I mean the prophecy was right... I *am* going to save the world!"

"Actually the second part of the prophecy

didn't say you *would* save the world," corrected the rarewolf. "It said you were the only one who *could*. And let's face it, Kingdomland still burns."

"Fine, who shall we save next?" said Frog. "I've got enough mightiness to go around!"

"No offence, but I've had enough of heroism to last a lifetime, truth be told," said the bragon. "I need a cup of tea…"

"They're right, Frog," sighed Kryl. "You were very brave and yes, very mighty. But the Kroakans have overrun this world and we have one box of talismans left. We need to hide. It's the only way we'll survive."

"Come on, you must believe in the prophecy after all my champion business?" he asked. There was a long moment of silence. "*Wait a minotaur*, does *anyone* believe it?"

"Well…" muttered the bragon.

"The thing is…" added Kryl.

"I *thought* I did…" sighed the rarewolf.

"Baa," said Sheriff Explosion.

"Yoiks," Frog sighed. "None of you believe I can save the world?"

"I b'lieve it," said a small voice.

Frog turned to see Princess Rainbow standing in the doorway. "I b'lieved you could save my mummy and daddy and you did. I b'lieved you could stop the ay'lun space invaders and you did. With help from all of us and especially me, because I'm a princess."

She smiled a toothy smile.

"And I b'lieve you can save the world, too."

Frog heard explosions echoing through the air … the grating hum of traceships … the shriek of sunder-beams … the rumble

of sunder-storms ... the sound of the End
of the World.

He took a deep breath.

"So do I," he said with a grin. "Let's get
started."

Nigel's Guide to
Bragging

Step One

A wise old bragon once said, "If no one's around to hear your bragging, does it even make a sound?" To fill yourself up with hot air, you'll need someone to listen to your boasts, by gosh! Oh, you might feel awkward telling everyone how thoroughly brilliant you are (and yes, they'll eventually want to punch you in the face) but remember: if you don't boast, you don't fly ... and a life without flying is a load of old smell.

Step Two

Start small. Big boasts on an empty stomach are a recipe for trapped wind. You may want to jump in with both claws, but you'll inflate too quickly and end up farting for a week. And you'll still be stuck on the ground! Build your bragging slowly at first – start by giving yourself a nifty title (The Duke/Captain Admiral/Glorious Victorious/Beverley Superbest) and then focus on how colourful, shiny and toothsome you are.

Step Three

Time to get serious, by gosh. A steady flow of boasts is essential for proper inflation. Use your surroundings for inspiration ("The Duke could out-run that horse! The Duke could out-swim that fish! The Duke could out-smell that flower! And that one! And that one!"). It helps to address your audience directly, especially if you're telling them why you're much, much better then they are.

Step Four

Don't wait, inflate! Keep the boasts coming thick and fast by awarding yourself as many impressive titles as possible – a quick fire list will ensure rapid expansion ("Behold, the Tremendous Truth Trumpet, Major Magnitude, The Greater Still, Noble-Head the Fantabulous..." and so forth.).

Step Five

Up, up and away! Once you're filled with hot air, you'll find yourself floating into the sky. Use your wings to point you in the right direction and control your descent with careful burps. Yes, your parents might tell you burping's rude but it's the only thing that will stop you floating up into the sun! On the other hand, a really big burp will leave you totally airless ... and it's a long way down. Follow this simple rule, by gosh: the bigger the belch, the bigger the squelch!

The Advenchur continues in

THE MIGHTY FROG

Coming in 2015!

Hear is a bit of what happuns after the stuff that just happund

...And so roomers spred abowt a misterious Kroakan rebul who was stopping the invaiders with all his might. He appeared misteriously from the darkness when the invaiders least expected it. He started saving the world one bit at a time. He did so much defeating that his lejend spred like butter on a hot turnip.

He was so mighty no one could stop him. He was so mighty he could not even stop himself! And he was getting mighterier by the minute...

The Rebel

"Who's there?"

The Kroakan sentry drew his sunder-gun. He peered nervously into the darkness of the forest. "Show yourself, in the name of King Kroak!"

"It's me, you slurm," came a cry. "Put that away before you hurt someone!"

"Kroop?" whimpered the sentry. From behind a blackened tree emerged another Kroakan. The otherworldly pair looked all but identical, with green skin, wide, hairless heads and bulbous, amphibian eyes. They even shared the same sleek, oil-black armour, which glinted in the light of the three moons.

"Of course it's Kroop! Who did you expect, King Kroak?" said the second

Kroakan. "Your shift is up, Krud."

"You're my relief? What a relief! I almost ... relieved myself," said Krud, sighing with relief. He pointed to the ten saucer-shaped spaceships parked behind them in a clearing of the forest. "Security of the fleet is all yours, Kroop ... and not a mikron too soon. I hate sentry duty — something about this planet gives me the slurms."

"You worry too much, Krud," said Kroop. "We'll have this mud ball conquered in no time. The natives are always trouble at first, but they come around soon enough. And if they don't, we destroy them. The system works!"

"It's not the natives I'm worried about," said Krud with a shiver. "It's him."

"'Him'? Oh, Kroak's Elbow, not this again," sighed Kroop. "I'm not listening to any more of your guff, Krud. This 'rebel' of yours is a myth."

"But what if the legends are true? What if he's the lost Kroakan prince, fighting against his own army, picking off our squadrons one by one?" whimpered Krud, his eyes darting frantically about. "They say he appears at night, riding on a thundercloud... They say he's taller then a thorg, with arms as thick as a zerk's tentaclaws, eyes redder than a grox's left buttock and legs longer than a flooble's—"

"Guff! Your brain's in a stink," tutted Kroop.

"—And fire breath and mind control and acid for blood!" added Krud.

"Would you shut your communication hole?" Kroop snapped. "For the last time, there is no—"

CRACK!

The snapping of burnt twigs was enough to make both sentries draw their sunder-guns.

"It's him! It's the rebel!" cried Krud. "He's come to show us the folly of war by killing us!"

CRACK!

CRACK!

"Shhh! It's ... it's coming closer!" hissed Kroop, aiming at the trees. "Set guns to sunder! Prepare to—"

"Baa."

From the tree line emerged a grubby mess of wool and legs. Krud and Kroop breathed a mutual sigh of relief.

"What is it? Looks like a puff of smoke," noted Krud, peering at the curious creature.

"Baa," said the creature.

"Whatever it is, it doesn't seem to be doing any harm," noted Kroop. "Let's blast it to atoms."

"Baa?" the creature bleated, staring blankly.

"'Rebel' indeed! You really need to get your brain unstunk, Krud," Kroop laughed, aiming his sunder-gun at the creature. "OK, on three. One ... two..."

BOOM!

The sentries spun around, their ear hollows ringing from the sound. The traceships were ablaze. They exploded one after the other, collapsing like dominos, metal screeching against metal, torrents of flame belching into the air. In seconds, all the sentries could see was fire.

"Green alert! We're under attack!" screamed Kroop. "Open fire! Destroy everything that's not already destroyed!"

As if on cue, sunder-beams streaked out from the inferno, blasting the sentries' weapons from their hands. A moment later, a figure emerged from the heart of the blaze. He was clad in leather armour and a long cape, which burned and smouldered. In one hand he wielded a sunder-gun, and in the other a gleaming sword. And his skin…

His skin was green.

"The rebel prince! He's come for us!" squeaked Krud. "And he's shorter than I expected!"

Kroop and Krud watched in horror as the figure strode towards them, flames licking at his ankles.

"You – you don't scare us!" cried Kroop.

"We are Kroakans! We are fearless! We—"

"We surrender!" Krud pleaded. "Please don't kill us!"

"I'm not going to kill you ... I'm going defeat the bumbles out of you," came the reply. "And then I'm going to defeat the bumbles out of your whole invasion."

"What are you?" whispered Kroop.

The rebel glared at him, reflected flames flickering in his eyes.

"I am Frog," he growled. "Or Frog the Mighty, or The Unforgettable Frog, or The Frog of Steel, or Frog the Defeatinator! ... Yoiks, I dunno, which sounds best?"

"Baa..." sighed Sheriff Explosion.

Also available:

GUY BASS

The
LEGEND
of
FROG

Have you read?

Join a mad professor's forgotten creation on the
biggest adventures of his almost-lifetime...

Guy Bass is an award-winning author whose children's books include *Secret Agent: Agent of X.M.A.S*, the *Dinkin Dings* series and the highly acclaimed *Stitch Head* series. In 2010, *Dinkin Dings and the Frightening Things* won the CBBC Blue Peter Award in the 'Most Fun Story with Pictures' category. Guy's books have also won a number of local book awards.

Guy has also written plays for both adults and children. He has previously been a theatre producer, illustrator and has acted his way out of several paper bags.

Guy lives in London with his wife. He enjoys long walks on toast and the smell of a forgetful sparrow.